I0552389

# LOOK WHAT YOU MADE ME VOODOO

## A MALVEAUX CURSE MYSTERY (BOOK 6)

### G.A. CHASE

BAYOU MOON PRESS, LLC

Copyright © 2018 by G.A. Chase

First Edition 2018

Cover Art by Janet Holmes

Editing by Red Adept

ISBN eBook: 978-1-940299-60-0

ISBN print: 978-1-940299-61-7

All rights reserved. No part of this publication may be reproduced, stored in, or introduced into a retrieval system, or transmitted in any form, or by any means (electronic, mechanical, photocopying, recording, or otherwise) without the prior written permission of both the copyright owner and the publisher of this book.

This book is a work of fiction. Names, characters, places, and incidents are products of the author's imagination or are used fictitiously. Any resemblance to actual events, locals, business establishments, or persons, living or dead, are entirely coincidental.

Bayou Moon Press, LLC

# ABOUT THIS BOOK

*Look What You Made Me Voodoo* Blurb

With Kendell and Myles safely back among the living, the task of keeping Colin in his place has fallen to Sanguine Delarosa. But as hell's angel, can she resist the devil's charms? In order to keep an eye on him, she may have to get emotionally and physically closer than she imagined possible. With the love of Sanguine, he may yet be saved.

When Colin resorts to his old ways by stealing Kendell's soul, however, Sanguine must face the hard fact that he might not ever change. Meanwhile, the band, Myles, and the faithful dogs once again put everything at risk to rescue Kendell from hell.

Despite all of Colin's misdeeds, Sanguine listens to his master plan of relieving people from the inevitability of death. His offer of a partnership leaves her wondering if she could be instrumental in creating a better future for humanity—or if she should continue with the team's strategy for the devil's ultimate destruction.

---

*T*hree weeks into his experiment of living like a homeless person camped out in Lafayette Square, one thing became clear: he needed to make some changes in his life. Each time Colin Malveaux considered returning to his penthouse offices, he remembered the folders of documents that lay strewn across the floor. The mess didn't bother him, but returning to a life that no longer had any meaning did.

He casually watched a businesswoman in a smartly tailored gray suit as she strolled along the radial walkway. She was headed straight toward the stairs leading up to the statue of Henry Clay that Colin called home. When she was less than a stride away, he stood up, trying to make the ensuing collision appear an accident.

"I'm so sorry," he said. Fortunately, neither had ended up on the ground, but the physical contact had caused her to drop her briefcase, which he gallantly picked up. "Completely my mistake. I hope you're not hurt."

She brushed off her suit as if contact with the down-on-his-luck businessman had soiled her attire. "You might consider taking a shower. There's one open to the public at the Y. Have a blessed day." She scurried off at a pace that wasn't so fast he would take offense but was quick enough to prevent any further exchange.

He sat back down on the steps, having gotten the information he wanted. Nothing about the encounter seemed in any way out of the ordinary. *That one transitioned awfully fast from autopilot to snarky but helpful. Usually, I get at least a canned smile before the real encounter.*

He watched the early-morning rush at the coffee shop across Saint Charles Avenue clear out. Each person, from high-powered executive to day laborer, hustled to work with a paper cup. From a distance, Colin noticed the uniform stride of each worker. The whole scene appeared to have been choreographed. But from his experiments, like the one with the woman he'd bumped into, he knew if he encroached on them closer than ten yards, they would resort to unscripted caustic behavior.

Hunger was knotting his stomach. After so long enduring the nonexistence of time in hell, he'd grown accustomed to the freedom from eating and sleeping. He hadn't yet adapted to his body's routine. As much as he had longed for the passing of days and the bodily changes they brought, now that he was supposedly back among the living, the inconveniences bugged him as they always had in his past life. The irritation caused him to look back at his business tower. From the top floors, all he'd needed to do was push a button, and whatever he desired would be delivered as fast as humanly possible—which, inevitably, had never been fast enough for his tastes.

*That life of luxury isn't the answer—at least, not at the moment.* He stood on the marble stairs and brushed the dust from the seat of his rumpled slacks. His caricature of a recently fired businessman living on the street, afraid to return home, had served him well. People went about their day's activities without giving him a passing glance.

A couple was discussing the upcoming festival that would fill the square with music and revelers. Their conversation sounded rehearsed, but Colin had trouble identifying why he had that impression. It was something about how the guy answered without appearing to pay attention to his companion, as if he knew what she was going to say and already had his reply at the ready.

Colin walked toward the coffee shop. He focused on the people performing their morning saunter along the sidewalk. As he approached the single lane of traffic, the strides of those across the street became more random. He hurried between a BMW sedan and an old VW bug before the light changed to green. Even the spacing of the cars seemed intentional. If they'd been any closer, he would have had to turn his body to get between the bumpers.

The redheaded college-aged barista greeted him as he pushed open the glass door. "Hey, Mr. M. The usual?"

"Yes, thank you, Kassie." He watched as she wrote his name on a cup and started toasting his bagel. From across the counter, he was close enough to see that her movements seemed completely natural. Something about her voice reminded him of the woman who had been discussing the upcoming festival—rehearsed but pleasant. Neither woman sounded like the surprised businesswoman he'd intentionally bumped into.

Once Kassie had put the breakfast bagel with lox in the bag and thrown in a packet of cream cheese, he pulled his worn wallet from his pocket. The dance of handing her his card, her swiping it through the register, and him returning it to his wallet happened in a fluid motion that they'd been practicing but still didn't have quite right.

"See you tomorrow, Mr. M."

"Looking forward to it."

She never pursued their business interactions beyond short, simple sentences. In his previous life, his wealth and power had often loosened women's tongues. Colin accepted the double espresso from the guy making drinks behind the counter. As a bit player without any lines, the guy could have been a robot for all the emotion he put into his performance.

Colin left the comfort of the café for the street noise of an outdoor table and chair. Kassie was pleasant enough to watch work, but once she'd completed her part in the play, she seldom gave him a second glance. He took a bite of the bagel sandwich. The crunch of the toasted layer, the saltiness of the lox, and the slightly-too-wet cream cheese all tasted exactly as they had the day before.

He focused his attention on the trumpet player across the park as the musician began his daily set. Colin closed his eyes and listened to the man's rendition of "Do You Know

What It Means to Miss New Orleans?" Having heard exactly the same score for the preceding twenty-one mornings, Colin thought he had it committed to memory. So long as he kept his distance, the trumpet playing would be as consistent as a vinyl record, with each pop and hiss being the same each time. The one time he had approached the musician, however, the song he'd been working on took on a different feel.

"I've heard enough." Colin picked up the remains of his boring breakfast and dumped it into the trash.

With no business to conduct, no people to see, and enough money in his account to last a couple of lifetimes, Colin wandered the streets of the Quarter, searching for a more respectable place to call home. Sleeping outside next to the statue had been an interesting experiment inspired by a picture hanging in his office. The framed photograph of a lone vagrant on a park bench still haunted him, but copying the man's life hadn't answered any questions.

Colin spotted a For Sale sign hanging from the balcony of a grand creole mansion that was purported to be haunted. So much space had never been his desire. Only people trying to flaunt their wealth bothered with buildings so large they took a crew of servants to maintain. Not that Colin was above such ostentation, but now that he had no one to impress, the added space just meant it was a longer walk from the bedroom to the kitchen.

"I want something high enough that I can look over the other buildings, but in the Quarter this time. And no friggin' neighbors, or whatever you call these fake people you've got running around here." Though talking to himself might be seen as a bad sign, he didn't think he'd started losing his mind just yet. As a businessman, he'd learned that vocalizing his desires had a way of making them manifest before his eyes. Life and hell had a lot in common.

As he wandered down Bienville Street toward the river, he spotted exactly what he wanted. An abandoned brick structure, which looked completely out of place at the outskirts of a parking lot, had just been remodeled into upscale condominiums. Even though there was no sign out front listing availability, he walked into the main office as though he owned the building. "I'd like to see the top floor."

The construction manager wore a crisply tailored suit and a hard hat. "We're still in the construction phase. These units won't be ready until next spring."

Memories of his old life as a corporate raider mixed with his suspicion of still being hell's devil. "Your boss probably doesn't work for me, but his boss likely does. And even if that happens not to be true, I can assure you that it's my money that's paying for all this activity. If you don't wish to show me the top floor, I'm sure you can find someone above your pay grade who can."

Colin watched in amusement as the exchange had the desired effect on the man. As always, the transformation started with the eyes. The dull, lifeless, bored expression changed as though someone had thrown a light switch. Colin barely caught the flash of light as the man looked down at his blueprints. People always tried to hide the change in personality.

When the foreman looked up, his demeanor made it clear that Colin had gotten through to his jailor. "We're just putting the finishing touches on that unit. The far elevator is dedicated to the penthouse." The man opened the middle drawer of the desk and pulled out a set of keys.

*Now, why do you need those if the building is still under construction?* Colin had been involved with enough building projects to know when he was dealing with someone who had no clue about what went into such work.

Playing the role of a man didn't appear to come naturally to the foreman. He walked with his legs too close together as if unaware of how such a stride would impact what was inside the slacks. Once in the elevator, the man avoided touching any of the dust-coated surfaces. *You played the role better as an upscale businesswoman. Even in a suit, someone in charge of construction would project an air of command. Fearing getting dirty wouldn't earn you any points with your crew.*

Colin followed the foreman into the sun-drenched penthouse. The concrete floors had been scoured, stained, and sealed. The brick sidewalls and large industrial windows completed the look of the warehouse. Inside the grand space, sheetrock walls softened the feel of the condo.

"I'll have a list of changes for you before I leave. Have it completed by the end of the week. The bedroom will do for now. You can expect a delivery of furniture by the end of the day."

Having found a place to lay his head that would be out of the elements—and even better, free from the constant reminders of the staged play of life—he headed to the river for a little contemplation. Talking out loud had its uses when he wanted something from the universe, but keeping the words inside his head carried with it the secrecy he needed to construct his plans.

*The likelihood that I am still in some make-believe existence grows by the day. But I need to be careful not to let whoever's watching know of my suspicion. Since chasing Kendell got me out of the swamp witch's version of hell, I have to conclude that this place is that sexy guitarist's doing. I have to hand it to her—she really had me going. The responses I've been getting to my random encounters, however, don't sound like her. She was never that good at hiding her true identity. So someone else, likely a woman, is guarding my domain. I have to assume nothing I see is real, at least not at a distance. No matter what reality they dump me into, I'm still the devil.*

SANGUINE HAD GROWN TIRED of mentally chasing Colin around New Orleans. Her network of animal spies—from mosquitoes to gators—kept her well-informed of his location, but it was still up to her to commandeer the closest voodoo puppet person in order hear what he had to say and keep him entertained.

Talking with Kendell at the seventh gate inside Delphine de Galpion's Scratch and Sniff perfumery provided one of the few welcome breaks in Sanguine's day. "I hadn't meant to provide him such a comfortable place to stay," Sanguine said, "but outside in that damn park, he was running me ragged. I really thought he'd have gone for that old mansion. Too bad. It would have been fun haunting his nights."

After nearly a month back among the living, Kendell had

lost the dark circles under her eyes. Her hair had regained the shimmery black punk-grunge styling that was meant to give her a hard edge but lacked the authenticity of the greasy-sweaty look she'd developed while in hell. "You know you could always come home. Just say the word, and I'll have Myles sneak through Guinee to open the door for you."

The escape plan was looking more inviting by the day. "It's not time yet. If he suspects what we're up to, he's proving awfully cagey about making a move against us."

"We did hear him say he realized he was in hell. Do you think he meant it, or was that just idle speculation on his part?"

Sanguine wasn't sure what to think. "He made the statement after leaving his office for the last time. He's been a little unfocused about what he wants to do. Maybe the words 'still in hell' referred more to him being lost for a direction to his life. With Colin, anything's possible."

"All the more reason for you to take a break. We can watch him from this side of the seven gates."

Having Kendell be so pushy about leaving actually helped Sanguine dig into her position. "Can't do it. Even though we've upgraded his prison cell, once he figures out the game, I'm afraid we'll be once again trying to contain him, like trying to hold back a hurricane with a mop. The longer he thinks he's actually busted through to life, the easier it will be to control him after he figures out the truth. Besides, I can only eavesdrop on what he's saying if I'm occupying someone within earshot. And I can't do that if I don't have access to these cardboard-cutout people."

"Still no luck teaching your insect friends to understand English?"

The little buggers had had an easier time teaching Sanguine how to see the future. "Their ears don't work like ours. I swear, you'd think whoever designed insects was working in a different laboratory from the team focusing on all the other animals on Earth. Nothing about those little creatures matches up with how I use my senses."

"Speaking of which, what do you see?"

Sanguine rubbed her eyes. *As if normal human vision wasn't tiring enough.* "Peering through the glass marbles in those mannequins' heads has severe limitations." She spread her white ten-foot-wide angel wings. "And flying around after Colin with these would tip our hand. He is giving me a migraine with his self-doubt. If he'd just pick a direction for his life, I could figure out what he's up to. I swear, it's like he's taunting me with his indecision."

"So you think he's intentionally keeping us off guard?" Kendell's questions sounded too much like the voodoo-doll people that inhabited the virtual-reality hell.

"Probably, knowing Colin. How are things going on your side of the wall between the living and the damned?"

"About like you'd expect." From the way Kendell avoided eye contact, it was clear she felt bad about enjoying life. "Myles and I take Doughnut Hole and Cheesecake for walks each morning. Sometimes we stop at the café on Frenchmen for coffee and muffins. Most of the day, we're busy getting the Scratchy Dog ready for the night's activities. When the band doesn't have a gig, Polly drags me to as many clubs as she can to check out potential groups for our free slots. Running a bar and music venue while still performing with the band isn't as easy as it seems."

"Sounds boring."

"Well, the position of hell's avenging angel was already taken."

Sanguine wasn't in the mood for levity. "Any news from Myles's overlords?"

"Don't call them that." Kendell's sneer let Sanguine know she'd hit a nerve. "The voodoo loas of the dead were only trying to help. If it hadn't been for the gift of Baron Samedi's cane, we'd all be in a lot of trouble right now. I'm just glad Myles figured out how to use it to travel between dimensions."

"Fair enough, but I still believe they didn't give him their powers without some ulterior motive."

Kendell nodded. "I suspect you're right. This is why I miss you so much. You're one of the only people I can admit that to without causing a fight. I still set a place for you at dinner each night."

Sanguine could practically taste Kendell's crawfish étouffée. "You're a little temptress. Do you know that?"

"So I've been told, and by the devil himself. The band is playing a gig tonight, so we can keep an eye on Colin. You should take the night off."

"You think all five of you can cover for me?" The idea made her nervous. It wasn't in Sanguine's nature to hand off a responsibility to others.

"Myles will be tending bar, so technically, it'll be six of us standing guard at two of the gates to hell. Since we can each occupy our voodoo double, that's a lot of cardboard people for us to take over should we need to."

"And if he steps outside? You can only take over the mirror images of yourselves. Since you guys will be busy onstage, in both realities, you'll be like babysitters making out on the couch when you're supposed to be watching your charge."

"Even if he does leave the club, what's he going to do? Luther once again has full control of the World Trade Center. Without his little toys, Colin is just a dude wandering the city. It's not like he could kill anyone or punch a hole in dimensions."

Kendell's dismissive language showed once again how she never understood how dangerous their adversary could be.

"That's what you said after we built the seven gates," Sanguine said. "Look how that turned out."

~

AFTER HER CONVERSATION WITH SANGUINE, Kendell rushed home to snuggle against Myles on their couch with Cheesecake next to her and Doughnut Hole curled up on a pillow. Between spending the day readying the club for business and playing the late-night gig, she never had enough hours left for family time.

"How's she doing?" Myles asked.

Kendell often had to recount her talks with Sanguine to multiple people, but at least Myles didn't offer unhelpful advice. "She's tired. I had to mention her coming home before she started getting snarky. This plan of hers is never going to last six months."

"Are you afraid we're going to have to launch another rescue attempt?"

Kendell scratched Cheesecake's ear to calm the old girl down. Just the mention of her mistress returning to hell made the dog tense. "I can't see how it would do much good. She has full run of the place now. Every person we're projecting and every animal her grandmother created is under Sanguine's control. I doubt I'd even be able to step through the gate from Guinee before she'd bombard me with mosquitoes to drive me out of her realm."

"You do have a hatred for those little bloodsuckers. She would probably modify them to look like miniature vampires just to freak you out." He stuck his front teeth over his lower lip and flapped his hands.

"That's not funny." But Kendell was laughing in spite of herself.

"Just trying to lighten your spirit. Wish I could do the same for Sanguine, but then, she never really got my sense of humor."

Kendell rested her head against Myles's shoulder. "She needs a boyfriend like you, but I'm not giving you up."

"You're not fooling me. What she wants is you as her girlfriend."

Kendell turned so she could see his eyes. "Would you give me up if it meant bringing her home?"

There was a nervous tinge to his laugh. "Nope. Sorry. And just for the record, I wouldn't give you up to Colin either—even if it meant ending him as the devil. This whole reality can go to hell before I let go of you."

She settled back against his chest. "Hopefully, it won't come to that."

He caressed her arms. "You still feel bad about leaving her in charge?"

Her muscles relaxed under his touch. "Colin always finds a way of besting me. Even when I think we've won, he just comes back stronger. I fear I've become too predictable. Sometimes being a good team captain means knowing when to hand the game off to my best player. Sanguine guards her grandmother's realm like it's her mission in life. I can't compete with that."

"I thought we were working *with* Sanguine."

Kendell loved Sanguine like a sister, but that closeness too often resembled sibling rivalry. "Someday, when this is all over and Colin is no longer a threat, I hope she'll stop challenging everything I say."

Myles kissed Kendell on the back of her head. "You've been known to have an opinion or two about her plans as well."

"That's because she's reckless. If she didn't have me to keep her grounded, I don't know what would happen."

"You're still worried she intends to destroy him?" Myles asked.

She wasn't really worried about that. Sanguine could be difficult to convince, but once she made a promise to Kendell, she kept it.

"I think she understands why that wouldn't do any good. Though her explanation of different time lines confuses me, at least she has developed her own reasons for sticking to the plan. I'm more concerned about what she intends to do with him now that she's agreed to let him live."

~

MYLES GOT into his groove of serving drinks at the Scratchy Dog with his longtime bartending buddy, Charlie. Though Myles had been coerced into co-ownership of the club with Kendell, he had no illusions about who really kept the joint running smoothly. They'd be lost without Charlie.

"You expecting any extraordinary visitors tonight?" Charlie asked.

Myles watched Kendell tune her guitar and check the microphone balance onstage. The routine was her way of transitioning from Kendell Summer, voodoo practitioner and guardian of the seventh gate to hell, into Olympia Stain, lead guitarist for Polly Urethane and the Strippers.

"With Kendell's magical guitar pick in hell and my cane again locked away in my safe, I'm hoping for a quiet night— paranormally speaking."

"Good, because there's a sorority convention in town," Charlie said. "Things are going to get busy fast."

Even in a sexually open city like New Orleans, the prospect of a large influx of women made Charlie strut around behind the bar like a peacock displaying his feathers. There was a time when Myles would have been filled with the same anticipation.

"You know the drill," Myles said. "No leaving early, no matter how cute she is."

"Yes, Boss."

Though Myles enjoyed the nightly banter with Charlie and watching Kendell do what she loved onstage, his connection to hell put him on edge. For the most part, he left his doppelgänger on autopilot in Colin's world. But somehow Delphine had managed to copy Myles's more aggressive qualities when she created the voodoo puppet. More than once, he'd had to step into his representation to prevent a fistfight with the devil. That kind of double duty often made him screw up drink orders.

"I may have to step out a few times tonight," he said. "I'm sharing babysitting duties with Kendell and the band. My usual means of entertaining the brat might get a little challenged."

"You never were any good at doing two things at once."

The band had barely finished their first number before the club started filling with drunk, rowdy college girls. And where women congregated, men followed. For each convention, Charlie stocked the bar for differing levels of drink sophistication. With so many college kids in town, every fridge in the club was crammed tight with beer. Though the place got busier as the night wore on, the bartending end of things never got more complicated than popping open another cold one.

In the midst of slinging bottles, Myles sensed his doppelgänger losing control. Like a cell phone that kept vibrating in Myles's pocket, his double in hell tried not to be intrusive but somehow managed to need help at the worst times. "Cover for me."

Charlie didn't even break eye contact with the blonde he was serving. "Don't take all night."

Kendell cast Myles a worried look as he snuck around the stage out to the courtyard. All he could do was shrug at her. Until he occupied his voodoo copy, he really had no way of knowing what mischief Colin was up to. To Myles's surprise, his double was also sitting at the metal table out back instead of slinging voodoo beers with cardboard-cutout Charlie behind the bar in hell.

No sooner had he taken over his hell representation than Colin joined him from the bar. "Thanks for meeting me."

Myles did his best to keep his cool. "Seemed like a better choice than getting into a brawl in front of my patrons."

Colin set his rum and coke on the table. "I'm not looking for a fight, but I am going to continue coming to your club. Having you glare at me all night from behind the bar is getting tiresome. I won't insult your intelligence by saying I'm not interested in your girlfriend, but she has made it clear she's not interested in me. So really, if you trust her, you have nothing to be so cross about."

Myles really wanted to let his alter ego throw a punch at the guy. "You think I've forgotten about you possessing my body or any of your other transgressions?"

"Of course not. What I meant was, I'm not currently a threat to you. I'm not asking to bury the hatchet, just looking to make sure there's nothing disgusting added to my drink."

Myles would have been happier if Colin thought there

was a side of spit added into the mix. "I can't answer for how Charlie makes your drinks."

"So long as I know you're not influencing his recipe."

Myles never cared much for small talk, especially not with the devil. "You have my word. If there's nothing else, I do have a bar full of customers."

Colin raised his hand. "I do have one other minor request. In the interest of distracting me from pursuing your girlfriend, do you think you could see your way clear to arranging a meeting between me and Sanguine Delarosa?"

Myles wasn't sure how to answer. Though Sanguine did occupy the same realm as Colin, she had wings, and her eyes looked like faceted crystals. Those changes would be certain to tip him off that he wasn't back among the living. As the only other physical person in hell, she didn't have a fake body double for meeting with Colin.

"I'll talk to her, but no promises. Unlike you, I don't pass women around like trading cards."

"Of course you don't." Colin's comment was thick with sarcasm. "As a club owner, I'm sure all your shot girls voluntarily dress so skimpily. If you put in a good word with Sanguine, I'm sure she'll listen."

## 2

*C*olin checked his pocket watch. The band was well into their second set of the night but still had at least another hour onstage. He squeezed onto the dance floor and worked his way to a ravishing redhead. He'd been eyeing her all night. From the way she undulated with her arms over her head, she clearly wasn't shy about advertising what her body had to offer.

As Lincoln Laroque, high-powered businessman, he'd never had trouble bedding women. And as Baron Malveaux, he'd had brothels so filled with his conquests he could have partaken of a different woman every night for a year. But as Colin Malveaux, former devil and supposed recent escapee from hell, he'd discovered the meaning of rejection. Unnervingly, each woman he approached started off pleasant enough, but as the conversation moved from benign to seductive, their excuses all started sounding the same. The trick was to move in quickly and act fast with as little conversation as possible. With so many people pressing against each other, his jailor couldn't transition fast enough to keep up with Colin's advances. Once his jailor caught on to what he was up to, she invariably moved in to cock block him.

The band was playing "Lady Marmalade." Colin's dance companion was the definition of airhead. Every comment he made was greeted with a high-pitched laugh, even when he wasn't making a joke. Typically, to make sure he'd been heard, he would wait for the band to end a number before making his move, but those breaks were often when a woman would transform from a flirtatious sexual prospect to a repentant conservative opponent.

As Kendell focused on her vocals, Colin took the redhead's hand. "Let's get a little fresh air."

His companion again laughed as her reply—a reaction he took as acceptance. He walked out the door, and she followed him as if she were a balloon animal on a string.

After a half dozen of such encounters, he'd perfected his routine. The dark alley that ran alongside the club lacked the romance of a suite at the Royal Sonesta, but then, he never got a woman more than two blocks from the club before she tendered her rejection.

The sex was quick, unimaginative, and dirty. Her cries of orgasm as he pressed her against the cold, damp brick wall reminded him of an actress's fake moans in a cheaply made porno. He honestly didn't care. As soon as he finished, he headed deeper into the dark alley while pulling up his pants. He didn't bother seeing if she returned safely to the club.

Though the physical release helped clear his head, what

he'd really wanted to see was if she'd change personas. She didn't.

His conversation with Myles had started off rather stiffly, but once he was out in the courtyard, the irritating buffoon returned. What mattered most was that at no point did any of his acquaintances of the night exhibit the snarky feminine mystique he frequently encountered. *So you've taken the night off. I suppose you deserve it, but your exhaustion doesn't bode well for you.*

He slapped at a mosquito that had the nerve to suck his blood. He missed. "That's right—fly back to your mistress, and tell her of my whereabouts."

Just for fun and curiosity, he focused the same kind of attention on the retreating bug as he had on his bats in hell. To his amazement, the small creature turned around and flew at attention before his eyes. He squished the bloodsucker with a loud clap of his hands. "You really are tired, aren't you, my jailor? Interesting."

He held the thick dark-red splat up to a security light. *At least I'm real.* Like a vampire testing out a sample of blood to make sure it wasn't tainted, he put the tip of his tongue to his palm. The blood was still warm. It tasted like a demi-glace that had dripped off a steak cooked rare.

He pulled out his cell phone and punched in the number of his office. "Send a town car. I don't feel like walking tonight."

～

SANGUINE RUBBED her forehead as she listened to Kendell

recount the night's adventure. "Tell me again what he said to Myles."

"He wanted to meet with you, but Myles told him it would be your decision. Clearly, we'll have to tell him no."

She knew it had been a mistake to take the night off. "He suspects I'm up to something. While we were in hell, he saw me with my wings. He must think meeting with me will prove whether or not he's left hell."

"Isn't that what we want? Once he knows he's in hell, we can move forward with directing him toward the seven gates. According to Baron Samedi—since Colin, in the form of Baron Malveaux, already died—the final gate will dump him back in Guinee, and then the loas of the dead will usher him into the *deep waters*. Having him figure out his situation wasn't unexpected."

Even after a night's sleep, Sanguine's mind wasn't as sharp as she'd have liked. Spending so much time in hell dulled her like a knife run against a rock. She closed her eyes and focused her attention on hitting each of the main points. "The seventh gate you watch over is between this hell and life, not Guinee. I don't trust anything those voodoo loas say. Even if he did end up among the dead, Baron Malveaux took over that purgatory once before. There's no reason to believe he'll just quietly accept the loas' judgment now. And if he does work through our gates, that doesn't mean he's been rehabilitated. He's already proven his ability to trick us. Having the devil walking among the living would be even worse than having him confined to hell. The ideal situation would be for him to accept this world we've built as his new reality—either because he thinks he's back among the living or because he sees this version as preferable to life. The longer he's here, the better our chances. Whatever happens, we need to know the instant he realizes what we've done. If he already knows—and we're again playing a game he's devised—we may be too late."

"What do you want to do?"

Sanguine knew it was pointless to say she wanted to kill Colin. The ongoing fight might give her a burst of adrenaline, but she needed support, not anger. "I need a better look into his life. Are you playing again tonight?"

"Yep, it's Saturday. You looking for another night off, or do you intend on breaking into his loft?"

*Are you crazy?* Sanguine resisted telling Kendell what she thought of that idea. "Neither one. I'll be at the club. You guys just put on a kick-ass show, okay? I could use the entertainment."

Once Kendell signed off from the seventh gate, Sanguine wondered if she'd have the nerve to go through with her idea. She'd jumped into so many women to reject Colin's advances that having to accept one made her feathers quiver. *Sex is nothing more than a physical encounter, and it won't even be my body he's fucking. Basically, I'll be doing nothing more than watching porn. For me to know if he thinks he's still in hell, I need to see how he's interacting with this reality.*

The justification for her upcoming liaison, however, didn't ease the icky feeling that coated her skin like the residual slick after a swim in an oil spill.

FROM THE RECLINER in his condo, Colin had a perfect view of the World Trade Center. He restlessly rocked in the chair while twirling the plastic guitar pick he'd caught from Kendell with his fingers. Whether or not he was in hell wasn't the issue. Kendell and Sanguine had made a tactical mistake in letting him experience what it might be like to return to the living. Abject boredom wasn't his goal in life. Being the devil in hell, however, held real possibilities. And being the devil in *life*—now, that was a worthy pursuit.

*I don't even know what it means to be the devil. I've been so busy trying to escape that I never fully embraced my godlike powers.* He twirled the small triangular piece of plastic faster. What he really needed was to break back into Luther Noire's sanctuary. When he'd had control of the World Trade Center, he'd been as foolish with the paranormal objects as some idiot burning paintings in a museum to stay warm. All the practitioners of magic since the beginning of time had their life's accomplishments housed in that tower of concrete, steel, and glass. As an interdimensional embassy, the tower and its contents existed in whatever reality Colin inhabited. The treasures were there for the taking. He had no one to stop him, save for the one man who knew the true dangers. *Start slow. Avoid detection. Luther must be going crazy trying to round up all the vaults I jettisoned. He'll already be distracted.*

Colin threw the pick onto the coffee table to stop his fidgeting. Like an omen of good fortune, the piece of plastic stopped in the middle of the glass surface instead of skidding off to the floor. *My luck is changing. All I need to do is avoid whatever malevolent presence keeps foiling my advances.* "Show yourself, Sanguine Delarosa."

He didn't expect an answer. He couldn't even be sure she was the one pulling the strings on the people he met, but as the granddaughter of hell's architect, she was probably in charge. Asking Myles to set up a meeting had been more about calling the team's bluff than actually wanting a conversation with the woman. If he were to pursue his plan, he'd need a better way of keeping tabs on his jailor than bumping into random women.

"Guess I'll be making another trip to the club. Hopefully, you got some rest last night."

To avoid driving himself crazy, he spent the afternoon wandering the Quarter. He couldn't be sure, but it seemed every woman he passed eyed him with suspicion as if he were some rapist. Though as Baron Malveaux he'd indulged in such perversions, taking a woman against her will no longer carried any satisfaction for him. All such violence proved was a man's brute force and lack of self-control, not his skill. To seduce a woman, however—especially if such a dalliance wasn't in her nature—required finesse. He considered professing his innocence to an elderly woman who scampered past him toward a waiting bus. But admitting his suspicion that Sanguine spied on him from every passing stranger would be to needlessly play a card from his hand too soon. *The real game will be tonight. It is interesting, however, that she appears aware of the upcoming duel.*

∽

As dusk turned to night, Sanguine learned from her mosquito squadron that Colin was already at the club. She still wasn't sure she could go through with her plan, but the random encounters she'd allowed with Colin weren't as insightful as she'd hoped. Like most people, he didn't reveal to strangers what he truly feared.

Enough of the city lay between Bayou Saint John and the French Quarter that so long as she didn't aim high into the sky, her nightly flight would be hidden from Colin by the buildings. In addition, City Park lay between her and Colin, stretching from the waterway to the lake. Her flight over the trees and lagoons wasn't quite the same as being over her beloved swamp, but it was the best the city had to offer.

She flew low enough over the manicured marsh to see her alligators lounging in the reeds. "I envy you, hell gators."

Her biggest challenge while in flight was resisting the temptation to time travel. A little peek at the forward lens of her mulitoptic vision would move her into the future. Staring too long at the images that drifted off behind her would send her back in time.

She closed her eyes and focused on the beating of her wings. The cool fall air felt good on her skin and feathers. The exercise helped calm her fears. Colin might be physically stronger than any woman Sanguine might inhabit, but that was the extent of his dominance. She'd seen him sneak into enough back alleys with various sex-bots to know how empty his life had become. If falling for Kendell had driven him to long for life, maybe becoming infatuated with Sanguine would redirect his desires to hell. *What he feels for me doesn't matter. He's loathsome. I just need to find out if he's faking it. Guys are useless at subterfuge while they're having sex with a real woman.*

She spread her wings to their fullest and banked back toward the park. If she didn't check in on him soon, he might choose another sex doll for his evening's entertainment. She landed on the large limb of an oak tree overlooking the New Orleans Museum of Art. *Mentally, I may have to be jostled in the club, but at least my body will have this refuge.*

With her eyes closed, she focused her attention on the women in the club. Like a chess player contemplating her next move, she mentally touched each female voodoo doll to judge Colin's interest. He sat at the back of the club, wearing tinted glasses to hide his eyes.

She took the body of a petite blonde that could have passed as Kendell's younger sister. Dancing had never been Sanguine's strong suit, but showing off the woman's body didn't take much skill. If Colin noticed her, he didn't make it known.

Next, Sanguine tried a redhead with pale skin and too many freckles. Again Colin didn't seem to notice. A long-legged blonde at the bar was talking to Myles while Charlie looked on enviously. *Perfect.*

Sanguine took possession of the woman's body and stared into Myles's eyes. "Do I have your attention?"

A flash of recognition lit up his eyes. "Do you need me?"

"Just checking in. Don't freak out if I leave with Colin. And don't tell Kendell."

He went back to mixing a margarita without responding.

When Sanguine turned her back to the bar, she noticed that Colin had removed his glasses. She maintained eye contact while taking a long suck on the thin straw of her hurricane. He was out of his chair before she set the tall glass back on the bar.

He walked up and took her hand as if she were a teenager caught out past curfew. "Let's get out of here."

Though her normal response to such impudence would have been a slap to the face that would leave a nice red mark, she meekly followed him. "Where are we going?"

He acted as if he hadn't heard her. Once out on the street and away from the club noise, he guided her toward the alley. "I've got a nice secluded spot for us."

She dug her high heels into the pavement. "So that's it? You're just going to haul me out back and screw me? Not very romantic, are you?"

He let go of her hand and turned toward her. "Did you really think we were coming out here to talk?"

"I thought maybe you'd buy me something to eat first. Or are you on some kind of fucking schedule? Only so many hours in the night to fill your quota?"

He glanced at the neighboring businesses as if he'd never noticed them before. "Feel like some pizza?"

Though Sanguine was the only actual woman in hell, and Colin had been left to his own devices with the women the team had created, she wondered if he could possibly be that rusty when it came to seduction. "You're quite the one for foreplay, aren't you?"

"You know the problem with all you women? Too many questions. I swear, every conversation I get into, all I hear are mindless questions. If I truly thought you could carry on an in-depth discussion for more than five minutes, I'd take you to Commander's Palace."

"Challenge accepted. I hope you like vegetarian pizza." She had long considered what a man would put up with in terms of a first meal with a woman a good indication of his interest in her. Only assholes contradicted a woman's tastes. If he thought she was wrong about the food, she probably needed to find a different guy.

"Haven't had it in years," he said, "but I'm game."

The small restaurant was nearly empty as all the jazz clubs were in full swing. The quiet atmosphere was a welcome change.

"What shall we talk about?" Sanguine asked.

"Since we're not just going to go right at it, what's your name?"

Sanguine quickly accessed the woman's specifics. Every fake person in hell was a projection of a real human. "I'm Annie."

"And I'm Colin. It's nice to meet you." His response sounded way too patronizing.

"What do you do for a living, Colin?" She hated small talk, but it came easily while she was hiding behind the mask.

"I'm between gigs, but I don't expect that to last long. I'm currently following a strong lead."

She tried not to stare into his eyes to determine if he was talking about her. "What profession are you in?"

"I'm in acquisitions."

"As in hostile takeovers?"

He leaned back in his chair and looked her over in a way that made her skin crawl. "Not if I can help it."

"You're not very subtle."

"If you were looking to be wined, dined, and swept off your feet, you've come to the wrong part of town."

She bit into the slice of pizza, hoping the garlic sauce might prevent an unwanted kiss later. "I never said I was looking for romance, just a little pleasant conversation. You were the one who bet I wouldn't last five minutes."

"Fair enough. What do you do with your days?"

*Oh, I keep an eye on the devil to make sure he doesn't escape hell.* "I'm a student at Loyola, studying human resources."

"So that's why you're so focused on my approach. You're not preparing a paper on sexual harassment, are you?"

She washed the strong flavor of the garlic out of her mouth with her sweet tea. *If only I could do the same with the disgust you inspire.* "Just observing the mating habits of the male of our species while he's on the prowl." *No wonder I prefer women.*

He tossed the crust of his pizza slice onto the metal tray. "Tell ya what. I'll concede whatever time you have remaining on your five minutes. Dinner's on me at Commander's Palace anytime you say."

"Grown tired of my company already? Or are you too horny for rational thought?"

He scratched the stubble on his chin. "Would it make me a cad to say the latter?"

"It would make you truthful. I can appreciate that. But I'm not letting you fuck me in some back alley. Take me to your place, or go back in the club and find yourself a whore."

"And potentially miss out on seeing you dressed up for a fancy dinner? I wouldn't dream of it."

∿

SANGUINE WOKE up in Annie's body. The sunrise from over the Mississippi streamed in the floor-to-ceiling windows of the old brick warehouse. She had only checked out of the night's escapades a couple of times, and that was usually due more to Colin's annoying grunts than his sexual aggression. He was a brutish lover but not as hostile as she'd expected from someone whose essence was partly Baron Malveaux. She tried sitting up without disturbing Colin. Annie's legs felt like limp noodles. Sanguine had used the body as if it were her own. Poor doppelgänger Annie was going to be sore for days, even if the woman who provided the projection never noticed.

Sanguine could tell from Colin's breathing that he wasn't sleeping. *Just like a guy to wait and see how a woman reacted to a night of sex before showing his hand. This isn't some fucking game.* She got out of bed, not bothering to wrap a blanket around her body. He'd already gotten what he wanted. It wasn't as if she had anything left to hide. Having been raised a witch, she saw nudity as natural and not something to be embarrassed about.

He didn't interrupt as she inspected his dwelling. A black-and-white photograph of a homeless man on a park bench in Jackson Square was prominently hung in front of the couch. *Now, when and where did you pick that up? I would have loved to have been a fly on the wall during that transaction.* Though her bugs had kept an eye on him, they couldn't know what he was doing every minute of the day, and even when they were watching, they didn't always understand what they were seeing.

"It's haunting," she said.

"Even more so with you standing naked in front of it. I wonder how that vagrant would react knowing you were looking at him in such a vulnerable state."

She didn't favor him by turning to gaze at his naked body sprawled on the bed. "Are you referring to me or him as being exposed?"

"I suppose both of you. For two such opposite people, there's a mutual expression of openness that's hard to put into words."

She hoped she hid her feelings better than the man in the photograph, whose face so clearly displayed a state of depression.

"I would have thought you'd go with something more upscale."

"Why are you surprised I like the picture?" he asked.

She motioned to the condo. "This place must have cost a good-sized fortune. The photograph is nice, but you seem more like someone who would decorate to impress, not for your personal contemplation."

He got out of the bed and moved in close. "You might be surprised to discover what attracts me."

When his naked body made contact with hers, Sanguine

considered turning Annie's body back into a sex-bot, but she stuck with her plan. "Do you see yourself in the image?"

Sex the night before had been easier to ignore than his hands on her waist in the morning light.

"I think it represents all of us," he said. "No one really feels like they belong."

*I belong.* "Sounds like something a man who was trying to convince a woman of her lack of worth would say. If you think I'm going to become your submissive sugar baby, you're dead wrong."

"I didn't mean to offend. When I bought the piece, I was at a low point in my life. I keep it here to remind me not to give up."

*Does that mean you're still trying to escape?* She couldn't be sure he even knew he was in hell. "I have trouble envisioning you sinking to the point of that homeless man. What hardship could you possibly have endured that you think would compare to this wretched soul?"

"For someone who spent the night, you don't seem to like me very much."

She was letting her irritation get in the way of what she needed to know. "I wasn't the one who just wanted to get it on without knowing each other's name."

"True. But I didn't lie about my intentions. I'm beginning to wonder if I'm being set up. You're not casing the joint for a theft, are you?"

*I already own it all, you fool.* "Just trying to get to know you better."

"That would imply you expect more of a relationship

than just the one night. I'll confess that I would welcome that prospect."

"You do owe me a fancy dinner. But don't get any ideas that last night will happen again. Just because you seduced me once, that doesn't entitle you to a free ride whenever you like."

He finally took his hands off her body. "I think you've made your position clear. But we are naked now."

"A situation I intend on rectifying. I have a class to get to." She grabbed her clothes off the couch and started getting dressed.

"At least tell me your last name and how to reach you."

*Fat chance.* "How do I know you're not some kind of stalker out to take advantage of me once my back is turned?"

"So I'm just supposed to sit here and wait for your call? Even you must realize that's not my style."

"How you normally conduct your affairs isn't my concern. I was curious about you, but if you keep up your aggressive pursuit, I'll know all I need to know."

## 3

*G*rateful to be back in her own body, Sanguine stripped off her goddess dress, flew out to the middle of Lake Pontchartrain, and dove in. Though she didn't believe she had any hang-ups about sex, apparently doing it with the devil—even if it wasn't her body—had crossed a line she didn't know existed. The water felt good against her skin, but her wings made it hard to swim. Like a waterlogged bird, she flapped against the top of the water until she figured out how to ride above it like a swan. *Kendell's going to be pissed that I didn't check in last night. I only hope Myles knows how to keep his mouth shut.* She swam a gentle breaststroke while spreading her wings to dry in the sun.

Though there was work to do, she needed time to think. Even if she didn't tell Kendell about the sex, her friend would still want an update on what Sanguine had learned from her evening with the devil. And so far, she had data but no answers.

She found it difficult taking off from the water, but once airborne, she was back in her element. And as awkward as the dip in the lake had been, it had washed her discomfort away. The ickiness of having had sex with Colin —even if only mentally—no longer filled her with self-loathing.

What she really needed was someone to talk to. The temptation to keep on her current path toward the swamp carried with it the danger of going back in time. Her grandmother would understand, but she was dead, and traveling back to tell her about what had happened might too easily create a rift in time that Sanguine wouldn't be able to bridge. *I need someone who understands Colin but won't tamper with this current reality.*

Of course, being the only person in hell other than the devil himself kind of limited her options. As she wasn't a part of one of the embassies, demanding a meeting with the voodoo loas in Guinee or Luther Noire in the World Trade Center was out, not that she wanted to talk to any of those dicks anyway. That left the guardians of the seven gates to hell. Though she could talk to Kendell, Myles, or the band, it was sure to be contentious, and she wasn't looking for a fight. That reduced the possibilities to people in other dimensions. Mary was a lovely lady but not the easiest to entice out of her comfortable plantation home in her parallel reality. And now that Colin had passed her first gate to hell, she had no reason to cross over. Serephine and her brother, Antoine, were just children. That left only

Fleurentine Laurette-Malveaux, deceased wife of Baron Malveaux.

Sanguine leaned her body to bank away from the swamp and back toward the city. The convent wasn't just a set of buildings. The compound was both the repository of the third gate to hell and an interdimensional embassy, so time had a way of warping around it. Miss Fleur had died before Sanguine's grandmother had built hell. If Sanguine could convince the nuns that her mission was worthy of their help, they could summon Fleurentine from the time she'd lived in their convent. Hopefully, the sisters would be less hostile than when Sanguine had petitioned them to help her save Kendell from danger. Appearing as an angel would have to be less offensive than barging in the front door as hell's swamp witch.

But first she needed to find her dress. According to the Church, even angels should be clothed. Sanguine flew in low over the city to avoid being seen by Colin. Though it would be easy to glide in over the convent's walls, pissing off the sisters wasn't going to help her cause. Miss Fleur would be hidden away in the past, and only the Reverend Mother had the tools to call her forth.

*Here goes nothing.* Sanguine knocked on the solid wooden door, feeling like a trick-or-treater begging for candy from the ghosts of a haunted mansion. Hunching her wings only made her more self-conscious of the new appendages.

The door opened just wide enough for half of the nun's face to show. "What now?"

"I'm here to see Miss Fleur. I need to talk to her about her ex-husband, the man we now know as Colin Malveaux."

The door opened a smidge farther. "What's with the wings?"

"Would you believe me if I said I was getting ready for Halloween?"

Though the woman didn't laugh, Sanguine saw the cowl of her habit quiver. "You'd be the first dressed-up reveler to knock on our gate in a century. Wait here. I'll talk to the Reverend Mother."

With the gate once again closed, Sanguine summoned a horde of mosquitoes, hoping to get an update on Colin. To her surprise, they'd lost him.

COLIN WATCHED the traffic along Decatur from his bedroom window while he considered what he knew about the women who were toying with him. Since being supposedly released from hell, he'd only run across Kendell at the club, and only once had she favored him with a conversation. He felt pretty certain he'd only dealt with her in her physical form. He knew what her personality was really like, no matter how hard she might try to act out another role.

Sanguine, however, appeared just the opposite. "Are you out there somewhere, playing with me like a girl dangling food into a terrarium to make a lizard move, or are we playing hide-and-seek inside my cage?"

Out on the street, tourists and businesspeople took on their usual choreographed performance. If this was still hell, someone was using a lot of energy to project the deception, and energy was something Colin understood. Even though he doubted anyone was looking, he tried hard not to stare at the World Trade Center for some indication of its role in his reality. *Even if they are using the power that I created to move these marionettes around my city, that wouldn't explain how Kendell and Sanguine have been able to interact with me. Assuming this is still hell—and I haven't simply lost my mind— neither of them should be able to project their spirits into this closed-off dimension.*

Of the two women, Kendell's presence was easier to explain. If her body was really just another of the walking and talking puppets, then she could use her voodoo powers to play her little mind games on him. That would require an object left in his realm—one linked to the curse. *She must have left that golden guitar pick in Delphine's shop. That's the only explanation as to why my plan failed and I ended up here instead of following her back into the land of the living. Two can play at that voodoo game.*

He waited for half an hour after Sanguine in the long-legged blonde's body had left his loft. Then he exited the building. He hadn't meant to piss her off, but he also wasn't overly concerned about her feelings. Women who'd become angry after having sex often turned their backs on him—literally and figuratively. They had a way of returning once they'd cooled off. Intense hate could lead to fiery passion, but boredom never led anywhere. Her inattention worked in his favor, but he needed to be sure she wasn't lurking about in any available body before proceeding.

The morning sun of the crisp October day felt good on his skin. After spending so much time in a post-hurricane, perpetual-night apocalypse, he had begun to fear he would grow gills and become the city's swamp monster.

Though he'd committed the paper to memory, he pulled out his notes regarding the contents of the World Trade Center. He might only get one shot. Luther Noire wasn't the type of guardian to allow a weakness in his system to remain once it was detected. Though Colin didn't need the entire contents of the building, even sneaking a relatively small vault out of it would be a challenge.

He folded the page, stuck it back in his shirt pocket, and turned away from the business tower on the riverfront. Though he only had to walk a couple of blocks to Saint Louis Cathedral, he used the stroll to interact with as many people as possible. With each encounter, he grew bolder. Not a single person transitioned to the snarky swamp witch.

Baron Malveaux had donated money for the grand doors of the church. Colin ran his hand along the wood, wondering if the diocese had any idea of what he'd really purchased. As if they were automated doors just for him, the huge slabs of carved wood opened without needing to be pushed.

He stood in the vestibule, wondering who would emerge from the side office. It wouldn't be Sanguine Delarosa— either in the flesh or as a spirit occupying another body. As an interdimensional embassy, the church would only allow a select few of its emissaries to talk to the damned.

Colin walked into the sanctuary, and the doors closed behind him. This wasn't his domain, but as with the World

Trade Center, he would never be denied entrance no matter the dimension he occupied.

He had met Brother Aramis enough times to recognize the man's heavyset physique under black robes tied with a golden sash. Even with the cowl pulled over his head, the monk was recognizable.

"I'm here to cash in on my investment."

The monk didn't even bother lifting his hood. "Donations don't work that way."

"I'm not asking you to do anything for me—no absolutions or pardons from hell. In fact, what I want barely has anything to do with the Church at all. There's something on your grounds that I need to access."

The cowl moved, indicating the man's nod of understanding. "You want to release the World Trade Center's vaults."

"Not all of them. As hell's onetime devil and the former controller of the building, I have a right to the fail-safe."

Brother Aramis appeared to float as he walked in the long robes that draped over his feet. "A member of one embassy, past or present, is allowed only entrance to other portals, not rights to their secrets."

"The fail-safe doesn't belong to you. It's part of the World Trade Center's security system. *You* are the one who doesn't have any rights to it, just as you don't have any justification for denying me access."

The man finally lowered his cowl to reveal his bald head. "What makes you think I have access to the fail-safe?" He was clearly under the false impression that only Luther and the archbishop could operate the hidden device.

*Because in this hell, I changed the rules when I controlled the World Trade Center. But the less you know, the better.* Colin tried to maintain a calm exterior to hide his yearning for what lay beneath their feet. "All I need from you is to open the crypt. I'll do the rest."

The monk walked between the pews. "Before I let the devil into our basement, come sit with me for a moment. It's not often I get to talk to someone who's been to hell."

Colin suspected the man was intentionally wasting time, but he didn't see much choice. *Perhaps humoring the cleric will soften him to my demand.* "What shall we talk about?"

"I'm curious as to why you think you've been condemned."

He sat on the uncomfortable wooden bench. "You expect me to confess my sins?"

The man let out a dry, raspy laugh. "Nope. Confession requires contrition. I expect your discussion of your transgressions will be closer to boasting."

*Probably true.* "Where do you want me to start?"

"Most people begin with the small stuff and build up to the grand offense. Usually, those confessions are more of a legal nature than a moral one and carry with them a lot of justification regarding why the sinner killed, stole, or what have you. I find delving into the seven deadly sins more instructive."

Colin barely remembered the term, let alone what the sins were. "I was never much for church school as a child. You'll have to enlighten me."

"The first is pride."

He stifled a laugh. "Is it pride if my accomplishments are

real? Any businessman worthy of the title embraces his successes. Sounds like an outdated sin to me."

"I suppose, as someone who took over Guinee, even for a short time, you would have needed an overabundance of self-confidence."

Though Baron Malveaux had served as the loa of the seventh gate, Colin retained only impressions of that time ruling over the souls of others. "Making decisions about who was allowed to pass to the *deep waters* and who had to remain in purgatory required a degree of separation from those I judged. I would guess you'd call that pride. I considered it a necessity. For the purposes of your curiosity, I'd say I was the most prideful person to inhabit that realm."

Brother Aramis nodded slowly. "The next one is greed."

Colin shook his head in disgust. "Are you sure that one wasn't added to the list specifically for me? According to Agnes Delarosa, I was the culmination of my family's greed. I was bred to be who I am."

"And you feel no guilt about amassing so much when others have so little?"

He looked at the man in the long robes. "You think denying yourself earthly comforts is any better? What good does your piety do for others? I worked for a living. My efforts created jobs. Of course I benefited more than anyone else. I'm the tip of the iceberg. My wealth is an indicator of how the rest of society is doing."

"Most of an iceberg is underwater. The larger the society, the more bodies for you to stand on."

The hardness of the wooden bench made it difficult to sit in one position for very long. Colin squirmed to face the monk. "Someone has to be on top. It's not like this church isn't the grandest in the city. Seems to me that your religion is a little hypocritical."

The cleric looked up at the ornate ceiling. "We don't exalt ourselves. This structure is for the worship of God."

The last thing Colin wanted was to get into a theological discussion. "Whatever gets you through your prayers. As for greed, not many can rival what I've amassed. What's next on your list?"

The monk sighed. "Lust."

"Do I really need to talk about my brothels?"

He shook his head. "I suppose not. The sexual perversions of Baron Malveaux were well documented. I'll be interested to hear your take on envy, though."

Colin turned back to the church altar with the huge sculpture of Christ on the cross. "That one goes hand in hand with lust."

The monk looked up at Colin. "You wanted what your victims had—wives and children? You already had a family."

Though envy wasn't an attribute Colin wanted to acknowledge, it was a driving force he'd long ago accepted. "Their examples of peaceful family living drove me into a rage. Why should they have what I couldn't? My wife and children were strangers who occupied my house and lived off my fortune like pet dogs."

"So your lust and greed were little more than your way of acting out your envy? I pity you."

Colin grasped the back of the bench in front of him with such force that his knuckles turned white. "I never asked for your pity. Offer it again, and I'll leave, with or without my possessions."

"My apologies, but your reaction to envy is enlightening. You don't appear especially gluttonous, unless we're talking about women."

Colin eased back into the pew. "I've never denied myself any pleasure. If there's something I desire, like women, I want them all. Isn't that the basis for survival of the fittest? The strongest male gets to mate with as many females as he likes to pass his genes on to the next generation. If I take more for myself than I need, that helps cull the herd. The weak must not be allowed to survive. What you call gluttony, I consider a public good. Society is too bloated with useless people."

Brother Aramis clenched his fists. "You'll forgive me if the Church takes a somewhat different view of the indigent."

Colin shrugged. "Everyone does what they think is best. What you do only prolongs their agony, but masochism isn't on your list of sins, is it?"

"Fortunately for you, wrath is."

Colin looked the man of God over from neck to torso. "I suspect you might have been a brawler in your time. Is wrath an emotion you've dealt with personally?"

Brother Aramis relaxed his broad shoulders. "I'll admit that before coming to God, I had a bit of a temper."

"It's an easy sin to get wrapped up in, isn't it?" Colin asked. "While I was in the process of destroying a person's life or tearing down a competing business, the bloodlust was insatiable. I'd get drunk on the need to pull apart every one of their accomplishments until there wasn't a single brick standing on top of another. Even then, the feeling wouldn't abate until I was playing the game with my next victim."

To Colin's surprise, the monk looked at him and nodded. "I found boxing to be my first legitimate form of release for those drives. The church gym is what led me to this life of contemplation. On this sin, we understand each other."

"That's six. What have you got left for me?" Colin asked.

"Sloth."

Colin took a moment to consider the sin. Laziness hadn't been a concern for him since his days in school, but something about his current situation made him reconsider his recent activities. *Could I really be staying in this hell out of my own inaction?* "I suppose there's an inclination to sit back on one's laurels, though I can't say I remember taking more than a day off in my professional life. Six out of seven sins isn't bad, though. Guess it's enough to be cast into hell."

Brother Aramis pulled on the bench in front of him to stand up. "It's not for me to judge you in this realm. Were you my responsibility, I wouldn't have cast you in the role of devil. Fortunately for me, you didn't come here seeking redemption."

Colin began to feel hopeful. "I only want what belongs to me—Baron Malveaux's possessions that Luther Noire has locked up in his concrete tower. With the curse no longer active, the items have only sentimental powers."

"I suppose a few jewelry boxes wouldn't be missed."

*Might be a bit more than that.* But telling Brother Aramis all of his plans wasn't in Colin's nature.

It took both of them to lift the Holy Table off the door to the crypt. Even though he knew they were completely alone, Colin couldn't stop looking around the sanctuary to make sure they weren't being spied on. Together, they hauled the heavy slab of floorboards off the opening.

The smell of mold, dirt, and death made Colin's eyes water. "You don't have to come with me, but if you want to keep an eye on your holy relics, I'm not going to refuse the company."

Brother Aramis peeked over the edge. "The archbishop made me promise to follow you anywhere you went in the church."

The man didn't sound overly eager to comply with his superior's orders. Colin considered giving him an excuse to remain above, but if he had to descend into the death chamber, he didn't see any reason why the member of the church shouldn't have to accompany him.

"At least you'll be able to confirm that I didn't desecrate any of your holy forefathers." Colin climbed down the wooden ladder to the underground cave. The bricks that lined the walls were cold and damp. Coffins filled the alcoves cut into the sides of the chamber. He moved a few feet into the room so that Brother Aramis could join him.

"All the archbishop told me was the fail-safe was down here and to keep an eye on you. Any idea what we're looking for?"

Colin had found a drawing of the control board but precious little information about where the connection to the World Trade Center was located. "It'll be a console covered in switches and buttons. Luther isn't a big fan of computers, so it'll probably resemble an old-time telephone switchboard. Based on how many vaults there are in the World Trade Center, the fail-safe won't be small. I just hope he didn't hide it in one of these caskets."

Brother Aramis pointed toward deep in the crypt. "Luther's building was constructed in the 1960s, so there's no point searching this close to the entrance. The church has been on these grounds since 1727. Of course, this version of the building only dates from 1794, but we'd have to assume this crypt was part of the original cathedral."

Colin would have breathed a sigh of relief if it hadn't required him to suck in more of the dank air. He tried doing the math in his mind. "So no closer than a third of the way back?"

"Only if you're talking about the tombs. The holy relics reside in the farthest chamber."

*Perfect.* Colin tried not to let his fears get the better of him, but exploring a catacomb in hell had a way of putting him on edge, even if he was the devil. "Knowing Luther, he would have demanded the fail-safe be put in the creepiest section of the crypt. He never could pass up an opportunity to instill fear in anyone dumb enough to cross him."

"You're the one who wants his tie pins back. Personally, I'd just go buy new ones. You can't possibly expect me to believe their sentimental value is worth this exploration of the dead."

*There, you're wrong.* "I have my reasons."

"So long as I don't regret letting you down here." Even the clergy covered their asses.

"My relationship with the Church will remain unchanged. Nothing I've ever done has led back to the dioceses."

The cave grew darker, colder, and more oppressive the farther they walked away from the opening. Colin tapped on the tops of the coffins to make sure each echoed with the same hollow death note.

"Haven't you ever heard of the phrase *rest in peace?*" Brother Aramis asked.

Colin couldn't have cared less about the cleric's sensitivities. "In my experience, there is no peace among the dead until they're poured back into the *deep waters.*"

"Then how about a little common courtesy? You could at least pretend to honor my beliefs."

He regretted not giving the man a reason to stay above. With each step along the ground covered in bricks and roots, Colin grew more accustomed to his surroundings. In the distance, he made out the back wall of the chamber. "We're getting close to the end. Luther wouldn't have been so obvious as to put the fail-safe in the very back. What can you tell me about these tombs?"

Unlike the wooden caskets near the opening, the stone sarcophagi at the back of the chamber sat out in the open.

"Most are archbishops or other leaders of the Church. A few are notable members of the community who had been honored for their good deeds."

*More like for their patronage, but I gave up that honor a century ago. As I can see now, that wasn't a mistake.* He stopped

49

along the corridor at what he guessed to be the early 1800s. The simple stone sarcophagus under his fingers had a familiarity he couldn't identify. "I suppose it would be too obvious for Luther to have picked a grave of a practitioner of the paranormal."

"We've lost the information on some of these burial sites, but graves are sacred. I find it hard to believe Luther would have been able to con the archbishop into using one of these resting places. The antechamber with the holy relics is just ahead and to the left. You'll have better luck in there."

Colin got the familiar prickly feeling along the back of his arms that let him know he was being manipulated. "I want to open this one. The name and information are all smoothed down as if someone tried to erase their identity."

"Marble ages," the monk said. "Ever been to one of the cities of the dead? After a hundred years, it's damn near impossible to make out a single letter of the inscription."

"Those grave markers are out in the open. People have a habit of running their hands over them. These are underground."

Brother Aramis pointed at the neighboring crypts. "Sure, but these all look pretty worn down."

Colin made a comparison of his chosen marker to those next to it. Though they did all bear the same marks of age, the one he'd first touched had a grittier feel to it as if someone had taken a sander to the marble. "I'm convinced that's the one. Help me lift off the cover stone."

"I'm only doing this so we can put it back in one piece."

"Whatever calms your conscience."

The stone weighed considerably more than Colin had

expected. Even with the two of them, they were only able to slide it halfway off the tomb, but that was far enough. He looked over the stone wall of the grave and saw the metal board lined with unmarked switches and buttons. "Luther didn't do me any favors."

Brother Aramis held the stone to keep it from falling. "This is all on you."

*Of course it is.* Colin pulled out his sheet of notepaper and began lining up what he remembered with what he was looking at in the grave. Each multiposition switch needed to be moved to the correct setting like some monstrously huge Mastermind board, but unlike the game of pegs, Colin would get only one shot at getting everything perfect. *If I set this thing up incorrectly, I'll probably be whisked into some prison of Luther's devising. This realm is bad enough.* Carefully, he made his choices among the battery of controls. As he pushed the activation button, a needle sprang up and pricked his thumb. He pulled his hand out of the crypt and saw the small drop of blood disappear into the hole in the middle of the button. Other than the needle, the whole control board could have been a disconnected piece of junk, based on the lack of feedback.

He sucked at the small pinprick in his finger. The blood tasted different than it had from the mosquito. *If this damn machine decides I'm not the one authorized to access the vault, that acidic taste will probably be poison, and I'll drop dead in seconds.* He rubbed at what felt like a bee sting, but as he waited, the pain didn't spread beyond the tip of his thumb, and it gradually faded. His body pumped so much adrenaline that his heart and respiration tried to get the better of him. *I can't let this monk see my excitement at having lived through the test.*

Brother Aramis shrugged. "I guess the fail-safe doesn't work."

Colin breathed a little easier at hearing his companion assume the adventure was a failure. "Oh well. It was worth a shot. Let's get that slab back into place before you pull a muscle."

~

COLIN LEFT the church feeling like a new man. Working under the assumption that he was still in hell—something that became more likely with every encounter—he and his possessions were now in the same dimension. All he needed was some scuba gear and freedom from Sanguine's supervision to allow him to retrieve them. Once he had his connections to the curse, and thereby to the golden guitar pick that was still stashed in Delphine's shop, he could combat Kendell on his terms. With a plan for her in place, he let out a high-pitched whistle to call forth his mosquito squadron.

A dozen bloodsucking bugs zigzagged in front of his face, each laden with a red abdomen filled to the point of bursting. He pointed at the one in front of his nose. The insect quivered at attention. With a fingertip of this left hand below the flying miniature vampire, he delicately squeezed it between two fingers of his right hand until a drop of blood pooled on his waiting digit.

He put the drop to the tip of his tongue then spit it out to clear the taste. "Yuck. Next."

One after the other, the small bugs presented their catch to their waiting master. Each tasted as watery and insipid as the last. Like a fisherman waiting for the big one, he knew he needed patience.

As the final bug presented its abdomen, Colin hoped he wasn't imagining things again. The insect didn't fly as true as its mates, and its body was a darker red. In his excitement, he nearly squished the mosquito to get at its contents.

He savored the warm, rich liquid. It was like tasting a perfectly aged rare New York steak from an expensive restaurant after experiencing only day-old gray burgers from a fast-food joint. "Show me where she is."

The bug did its best to not outfly Colin's ability to keep up, but being so small meant the creature had to double back and fly in circles. Trying to see it made for slow going. However, once Colin turned a corner at the end of the French Quarter and spotted Our Lady of Mercy convent, he figured out where the mosquito was headed. He hopped over the church-school fence across the street from the convent and found a gardener's shed. Safely out of sight from any passing marionette spy that Sanguine might commandeer, he kept his eyes on the gate. *Guess I'll have to wait.*

∽

SANGUINE THOUGHT THAT FOR AN ANGEL, she should really

feel more at home in the convent, but sitting on a bench in the common room while the nuns looked for Miss Fleur made her antsy. The mosquito bite on her shoulder didn't help. Even in life, the little monsters avoided sipping blood from a swamp witch. Something had changed in hell, and it wasn't to her benefit. *All I did was have sex, Grandma. I didn't even use my own body. I don't see how I deserve penance for such a trivial action.*

She hoped the reason for the bug bite was as simple as payback from her grandmother. The other option was that Colin had regained control of some of hell's critters. The implication that he'd have not only figured out his predicament but also amassed his bug army put Sanguine on the defensive. *I knew I waited too long.*

The Reverend Mother escorted Miss Fleur into the Spartan room lined with benches and tables. Sanguine had met the old nun once while busting down the door of the convent. Hopefully, the wings would calm the woman's fears about having let a witch into her sanctum.

Sanguine didn't try to fold the new appendages tightly behind her body as she had while requesting entrance. "Thanks for letting me see her."

"I can give you an hour, no more. This convent doesn't reside in your hell, so your magic won't work here."

Sanguine wondered what the nun thought she was going to do. "I only want to talk. But to be clear, outside this embassy's walls is the realm my grandmother created. She wouldn't take kindly to seeing me burned at the stake."

The old woman's facial tick could have been interpreted

as either a sneer or a smile. "We're at a standoff. I'll be back to bring Miss Fleur to her room in an hour."

"Thank you, Sister."

Sanguine waited until the old bat was out of the room and the heavy rough-hewn doors had closed before turning to the frail old woman in the handmade dress. "Thank you for meeting with me. I can't imagine that talking about your ex-husband—or what he's become—can be easy for you."

Though Miss Fleur's body appeared about to crumble to dust, her eyes were a bright sky blue that reminded Sanguine of summer. "The Archibald I knew wasn't a bad man, just an ambitious one. If you can remind him of who he used to be before that evil voodoo queen got her talons into him, I'll be happy to help."

The woman had an inner strength and grace that Sanguine found hard to ignore. "I don't want to lie to you. I slept with him last night." In her mind, she could use the justification of using another body, but such equivocations didn't work with someone so apparently pure of spirit.

Miss Fleur sat on the uncomfortable-looking wooden bench. "Sit next to me. I let go of my claim on him a century before you were born. Did your liaison have any positive effects?"

Light filtered through the clearstory windows and gave Sanguine a feeling of quiet contemplation. "I think that may be why I'm here. I've considered him to be the personification of evil for so long that I can't tell the man from the devil. What do you remember about the man you married?"

The woman's soft voice matched the feeling of the room.

"I was only fifteen when I married Archibald. He was twenty-five. I thought he was so dashing, a real man of the world. My daddy grew cotton like most of the farmers in the South before the War Between the States. I grew up out in the fields, working alongside our slaves. History makes that time sound so different than it actually was, at least from my perspective. I couldn't wait to be rid of the dirt that had caked into my feet and knees."

Having grown up in the swamp, Sanguine knew the feeling. "I'll bet Archibald never spent a day of his life sweating, hunched over in a field."

Miss Fleur smiled demurely. "He was a city boy when we first met. A couple of times each year, my parents would take us kids into New Orleans for new clothes and such. As we were walking down Royal Street, I was so fascinated with the buildings all crammed against each other that I wasn't watching where I was going. I plowed right into Archibald as he was leaving the bank. You can't imagine how mortified I was—a dumb country girl messing up the suit of a fine young businessman. I could have just sunk right into the storm gutter. But that was the very last time I ever felt unworthy of anything. He took me by the hand as if I were some elegant lady playing the role of a pauper. I remember that meeting like it happened this morning. From that moment on, my life became a whirlwind of dresses, dances, and desires. He loved showing me off, and I hate to admit it now, but I did crave the attention."

Sanguine had never been impressed with any man who thought he could win a woman by sweeping her off her feet. "Sounds like he took advantage of an innocent young girl."

Miss Fleur's eyes grew wide, giving Sanguine some inkling of what she must have looked like so long ago. "It wasn't like that. At least, that's not the way it felt at the time. To me, he was everything I longed for. Marrying him was my way out of the fields. Though a ten-year age difference might sound like a lot now, he was still only in his early twenties. He worked hard at the bank but never felt he got the recognition he was due. When his parents died of yellow fever, we took over his family's mansion on Saint Charles. That money changed him." She looked to have drifted off into the memory.

"I've found that money just amplifies a person's repressed characteristics. No one really changes." Sanguine needed to know if there was anything about Colin worth saving, but she wasn't above manipulating the data against him.

"It wasn't the money that turned him evil. You'd think with so much, he'd have been happy to take life easy. When I gave birth to Antoine, I hoped Archibald would take the time to be a proper father, but then he met the voodoo queen."

The story of how Archibald became Baron Malveaux had been pieced together to Sanguine's satisfaction, but as most of the facts came from Delphine de Galpion, descendant of Marie Laveau, the swamp witch had a healthy skepticism about who was ultimately responsible.

"Did he approach her, or did she seek him out?"

"Does it matter? Madam Laveau was a well-established figure in New Orleans. At some point, everyone had dealings with her or fell under one of her curses. In

Archibald's case, it was both. After giving birth, I couldn't wear the sheer, titillating dresses. Showing off his young wife in risqué clothing had guaranteed Archibald entrance into high society, and with me staying at home to raise our son, my husband found he was no longer invited to the fancy parties. He didn't take his frustration out on me, but he did become more distant. Without me on his arm, he needed another means of accessing the city's rich and powerful. He and Marie were made for each other when it came to milking the rich."

Sanguine could just see Colin tossing aside a woman who was no longer of any use to him. "Is that when he started opening his brothels?"

"That was much later. He still wanted recognition within the bank and to be seen as a member of the elite. Inheriting his family's fortunes wasn't enough. He needed to make it on his own, even if that required a little voodoo magic."

"I'm aware of how he stole Baron Samedi's walking cane, but I got the impression there was a history with Marie Laveau that predated that first Mardi Gras parade."

Miss Fleur spread her milky-white fingers on the wood-plank table. "He never would have gotten on that float if he hadn't first become head of the bank. As he was rising through the ranks, death spread through that building like the devil himself was walking the corridors. With each opening on the ladder, Archibald moved one step closer to the president's office."

Sanguine bristled at the thought of magic being used to kill people for such blatant advancement. *A Wiccan witch would have known better.* "You believe he commissioned Marie Laveau to kill those who stood in his way?"

The sorrowful look in the woman's eyes could have been real or just a trick of the light. "I didn't know what to think. Out in the fields, I'd worked closely with my daddy's slaves. I considered them friends. They talked about dealing with voodoo practitioners like you would talk about seeing a water moccasin in your path. I suppose that's why I steered clear of my husband's business accomplishments. But even then, he'd maintained his humanity—at least as far as I could tell. I suppose that by the time he became bank president, he was already collecting women as payments for his loans."

"Then he helped fund the Krewe of Comus as the first Mardi Gras parade in New Orleans."

Miss Fleur grimaced. "Complete with a decadent high-society ball afterward. That was when Archibald cemented himself as the most influential man in New Orleans. He started to insist people call him Baron that night. What none of them knew was the title was as much about him stealing the loa of the dead's cane as his economic power over people."

"Did you attend the parade and ball?"

Miss Fleur looked around at the plaster walls that had become her home. "I took Antoine to see the parade, but Archibald preferred to go to the balls alone. I'm sure he had mistresses by that point."

"Sounds like you had a lonely life once he got what he wanted."

She rubbed her arms as if a chill had descended on the

room. "He still had his moments. Serephine was only two years old at the time of that Mardi Gras. He doted on that child. I honestly thought she would be his salvation. But once he got hold of the cane, he became obsessed with the lust for power. Honestly, I'm not even sure he cared all that much about having sex with those women he enslaved. He just wanted to feel his power over others."

Sanguine struggled to compare the different sides of Archibald to the man she'd slept with the night before. "Last night, I didn't feel like he was trying to dominate me—at least not any more so than any other man I've known."

"My understanding is Colin isn't completely Archibald. There's another side to his personality."

*As if men aren't confusing enough.* "Lincoln Laroque was bred to be the son Baron Malveaux dreamed of. Though he wasn't as cruel in his manipulations of people, that might have more to do with the times we're living in than any higher morality."

"And yet you slept with the devil they both became," Miss Fleur said. "I can't imagine why."

Sanguine stood from the bench and stretched out her wings to their full ten-foot expanse. "I suppose I like the challenge."

4

---

*C*olin hunched lower in the gardener's shed as the gate to the convent opened. He felt like a stupid teenager spying on a high school crush. But no angelic girl on two feet compared to an honest-to-god winged human taking flight. Sanguine took his breath away as she flapped off over the shed. He'd seen her with wings before, but that had been while they were in hell, and she'd been only a spirit without a physical body. He couldn't allow himself to jump to conclusions, but her presence as an angel in his world added another piece to the puzzle. The mosquitos had already confirmed with her blood that she was more than just a spirit. *We'll meet again, but at the moment, I've got too much to do to spend my time fantasizing about a human-sized fairy.*

He let out a high-pitched whistle to rally his mosquitos and aimed the squadron at the retreating flying goddess. With his spies keeping track of her location, he summoned the courage to exit the small, smelly shed. The odor of compost stuck to his clothes like the mud that caked the soles of his shoes.

Colin looked across the street with trepidation. In the hundred years Baron Malveaux had spent in Guinee, he'd never been able to dominate the spirit of his dead wife as he had with his indentured concubines. Thanks to Kendell and her boyfriend, those captured souls had all passed on to the *deep waters*. Colin's loneliness hollowed him like maggots eating a carcass. He could trace that feeling to the loss of those women.

Memories of Fleurentine as a young, innocent waif hadn't faded with time, death, or his imprisonment in hell. As she'd matured, he'd grown tired of her. With each woman the baron raped, he'd hoped to recapture that first night with his virginal bride.

THE BARON SIDE of him didn't want to approach the gates to the convent. Had he not known better, he'd have thought Sanguine was using his body against his will, but from his experience controlling Myles, he knew what was involved in a full-body possession.

Instead of knocking, he placed his palm against the rough wooden door. Hopefully, the nuns would deny his entrance, but he had to at least try to see his long-dead wife. *This is what I get for having sex with that witch angel. I let it mean something.*

The hinges of the massive door creaked like a woman

screaming as the gate opened. "You've been expected." The old hag in black robes stepped aside so he could enter.

"It's not my idea to be here."

She didn't seem to care. "I understand, my son. Miss Fleur is in the common room. I'll take you to her."

As he followed the old woman, he wondered if her greeting had been purely ecumenical or if she was really his mother, who'd been dead for more than a century. Either way, the woman gave him the creeps.

"Why do you keep this place so cold? I swear it's ten degrees warmer outside your gates. I know this is your interdimensional embassy, but damn. You could make a visitor a little more comfortable."

"Talking is forbidden outside of the common rooms."

*If you're not my mother, you sure do a fine imitation of her.*

She led him into the long light-filled room. A woman sat halfway down the row of benches.

"Is that her?" He didn't really need the confirmation, but even talking to the old nun was better than facing what he'd done.

"I'll be back in an hour." The old bat closed the door after her, sealing him in with the woman who personified his history of mistakes.

Fleurentine stood from the bench and moved into the sunlight so he could get a good look at her. The long blue-and-white dress matched her eyes and hair. As a spirit in Guinee, she'd appeared as the young woman he remembered as his wife, but in the convent, she looked older than the nuns.

"You've changed," he said.

She spread her arms and turned slowly to give him a complete view. "From what the nuns tell me, I'm approaching the end of my life. Though I guess that's pretty obvious."

Walking into an interdimensional embassy could land him in any time period the guardians picked. *Why did you choose a point so near her death? Was it to increase my guilt?* "How much have they told you about what happens after you die?"

She waved him to the bench opposite her. "I know Baron Malveaux will keep me in Guinee to play mother to the sex slaves he kept prisoner. I also know I'll be freed to move on to the *deep waters* when the time is right."

*Of course they told you.* "You were all freed eventually."

"Not by you."

She had a way of getting under his skin. Whatever his excuses, her counterpoints of truth always struck deep into his soul like a knife plunged into his heart. "True, but I haven't come to discuss what's about to happen to you. I was only trying to find out if you knew."

"My time in Guinee hasn't happened for me yet. Long ago, I learned to live in the present and not focus too much on the future. Living with you taught me that."

Talking with her was like carrying on a conversation with a hornet's nest—each sentence carried stinging venom. "I suspect it would be pointless to apologize for everything I've done to you. You probably wouldn't believe me even if I tried. I didn't come here looking for absolution."

"Then why are you here?"

"I suppose I'm trying to learn something about myself by

examining my past." He refrained from calling her his failure.

"Does this need for self-reevaluation have anything to do with that flying angel who was just here?"

Sanguine didn't seem the type to kiss and tell, even if it was to dump him in hot water. "Perhaps not for the reasons you think. My perceptions of good and evil have become so jumbled that I find it hard to choose a path. I suspect Sanguine stands at the crossroads, but I'm having trouble reading her sign."

"Ever thought of consulting those closest to you?"

He tried to imagine who would be close enough to help him. Everyone he knew fit into the categories of adversary, employee, or vanquished. None seemed like worthy advisors. "People tell me what they think I want to hear or what's in their best interest." *Besides, there aren't many choices in this hell of mine.*

"If you've come to me, that's a pretty sad last choice. I don't have a clue about your current situation."

He stared into her eyes, detecting a deception. She'd never been much good at lying. He couldn't figure out why she'd bother hiding what she knew. "What did you and Sanguine talk about?"

She relaxed her rigid stance and smiled. "So this *is* about that sexy angel."

"She's one of the few who challenges me, but I can't tell if her intentions are for my benefit or destruction."

"You never could read people. The more success you achieved, the more your power and money separated you from others. Without that connection, you were flying blind, emotionally speaking. No wonder you wound up in hell."

He wondered if she'd unintentionally let her knowledge of his predicament slip, or if it had been a calculated ploy to get him to reveal what he suspected. "I'm discovering a reawakening of those connections. As you might guess, I'm finding the experience a little disorienting."

"The man who offered his hand to a young girl who'd knocked him into the gutter is still inside you. There were moments in our marriage when the real you emerged—mostly, they involved our children. I recognize him in you now. I can't tell you which path to take, but I won't hold you to the past."

He'd never noticed how closely Fleurentine's eyes matched their daughter's. "You used to do drawings of Serephine and Antoine. I know it's a lot to ask, but would you happen to have one I could take with me?" He wasn't even sure why he wanted the picture.

Her smile was the same one she'd had when he lifted her from the street. "I knew one day you'd come back. I'll send one out with the Reverend Mother." She got up as if to leave and put her hand on his shoulder. "I would tell you to follow your heart, but you'd discount me as being emotionally foolish. Stop following the animalist path of clawing your way to the top of the food chain, and do what builds you and others. And if you can, find someone who will help you along your way."

~

COLIN CONDUCTED his usual tests of the strangers on the street to determine if Sanguine was keeping an eye on him. Like most of the women he'd slept with, she was noticeably absent after the event, but she'd start spying on him soon enough. He didn't have much time.

He carefully held the rolled-up pastel drawing of his children, hoping not to smudge the hundred-year-old chalk. As always, Fleurentine's advice about Sanguine had sounded overly emotional, but that didn't make her wrong —just naïve. He hadn't reached the pinnacle of success in two lifetimes and bested the loas of the dead by being predictable. Falling in love with the angel swamp witch would play right into the hands of those who kept him captive.

After entering his building, he passed up the elevator in favor of the stairs. The jog up to his condo helped channel his adrenaline. He opened the door, feeling a renewed sense of hope. Things were going his way, even if he couldn't identify the source of his newfound luck. He set the drawing on his coffee table. The thick paper uncurled next to the guitar pick.

It wasn't his newly acquired memento that excited him. Somewhere out in the swirling water of the Mississippi was a vault full of his possessions. He needed a boat and some diving gear, but he had to avoid being detected by Sanguine. *Women hate not being the one and only object of a man's desires.*

The objects in the iron box that had once belonged to the baron still carried the curse. Kendell had made a mistake in stashing her connection to the curse in the golden guitar pick given to her by the loas of the dead. Power equaled leverage, and she'd foolishly put hers in a box like a little girl storing keepsakes in a treasure chest. Reacquiring his link to the spell through the objects locked in the vault gained him a tactical advantage—though it still wouldn't be enough to let him walk out of hell scot-free.

The noise of the dry dock across the river caught his attention. A tugboat was being stripped bare for a repaint. *They must have what I need, but every person I see is a risk. Hauling scuba gear on the ferry would look too suspicious. I'll need to sneak over and steal the equipment.*

Between talking with Brother Aramis, waiting on Sanguine, and meeting with Fleurentine, he'd used up most of the day. The cover of night would work, not just for his stealthy operation in obtaining the gear, but also for his underwater excursion. First, though, he needed a boat to cross the river without drawing suspicion.

He spent the remaining hours of daylight nonchalantly walking along the river. If by chance Sanguine was checking up on him with one of her spies, she'd assume he was contemplating their night together. Allowing her to think she'd had such a strong impact on him could work in his favor. Tugboats, ranging from small barge pushers to ocean-going rescue vessels, worked their way upriver, but few docked along the French Quarter.

He fondled the roll of cash in his pocket. It would come in useful even if the people he met were nothing more than puppets. Money was such a basic desire that it worked even on the mindless drones.

A large tanker struggled to make the bend in the river. Once the behemoth was clear, a small pilot boat that had been following it like a remora chasing a shark broke off and headed for the wharf. *Perfect.*

Colin resisted the urge to run toward the small boat as the three-man crew tied it off. He needed to be patient. A captain probably wouldn't be open to bribes, but a mate on night watch might. He turned to the setting sun. The tanker had been late making its way upriver. Most of the larger ships had either dropped anchor closer to the gulf or traveled beyond New Orleans to the loading docks and oil refineries. As he approached the high-speed blue boat, he heard the skipper wishing his mate a good night.

Colin sat on a metal bench designed to provide rest to weary tourists who couldn't handle the heat and humidly of the walk along the river. He nodded at the two men as they walked past him.

When the late-afternoon shadows melded with the night, he got off the bench and headed for the small boat. The pilothouse was brightly lit, showing the night watchman lounging in a chair at the wheel. *He probably has to keep watch in case there's some ship captain who's in too big a hurry to wait until morning.*

Colin hopped onto the deck and quietly rapped on the cabin's window. The sleepy boat attendant woke with a bit of a start but smiled at seeing he had a visitor. "Can I help you find your way, sir?"

Colin pulled out his roll of bills. "I was hoping I could hire you for an hour or two. Nothing overly illegal—I just need to secure some diving equipment and retrieve a metal box that fell in the river. I can pay handsomely, but we'll have to keep our activities out of the public eye."

"I'm afraid all I can do is run you around the river. Diving isn't a service we provide."

Colin nodded toward the dry docks. "That's where the 'nothing overly illegal' comes into play. I just need to borrow some of their equipment. If it makes you feel better, I can leave an envelope with some cash for the rental."

The man looked across the river and nodded. "No need. Everyone who works on the river is pretty chummy. I know the night watchman over there. If you've got the money and promise we'll return the equipment unharmed, I think I can persuade him to help. I'd like a better look at that wad of cash, though, just to make sure our hypothetical excursion is worth the risk."

Colin thumbed through the hundred-dollar bills until the look on the man's face switched from skeptical to eager. "We need to go as soon as possible."

By the time Colin made his way into the cabin, the man had already started the engine. "Just sit on the back bench. I'll have the lines clear in a moment. I hope you're an accomplished diver. The river gets a little squirrelly this time of night when the tides change."

Colin had to hang onto the bench supports as the small boat plowed through the waves toward the Westbank. Though he'd made the crossing numerous times in everything from luxury paddle wheelers to run-down ferries, he'd never before been tossed around like a fishing float bobbing in the rapids.

The pilot shut off the running lights once he'd cleared the ferry terminal. "Though it's not unusual to have boats pull up at night, no use advertising. Once I tie up, give me five minutes to talk to my friend. A couple of those hundreds might help smooth my negotiations."

Colin peeled off five more hundred-dollar bills. "Just be quick."

"You got it." The man had the boat moored and was over the side before Colin's eyes had a chance to adjust to the darkness.

He tried not to stare at his watch. *No one is ever going to make me believe all minutes are of an equal measure. I've spent enough time in hell to know better.*

When he saw the two men lugging an oxygen tank and diving gear across the heavily steel-plated pier, he ran out of the cabin to lend a hand. "I'll have this stuff back in an hour, two tops."

The security guard nodded. "You'd better, or it'll be my ass on the line. I'll expect the second half of my money when you return."

Colin wondered if that meant a match to the full five hundred he'd handed the pilot. *The money doesn't matter.* Though he hated even the possibility of being taken advantage of, his prize was worth the cost.

While the boat lurched back across the river, Colin flopped around on deck like a catfish as he tried to squeeze into the wet suit.

"Where're we headed?" the pilot asked.

"You know the wooden pilings that support Spanish Plaza? What I'm searching for is somewhere under that built-up wharf."

The boat swung wildly away from the Quarter and toward the Crescent City Connection. "You realize there are a lot of tourists who find that overlook of the river kind of romantic. That bridge is not the most private spot for conducting whatever activity you have in mind."

Colin surveyed the area. "Drop me off upriver alongside the outlet mall. None of those shops have windows. I can float downriver under Spanish Plaza until I find what I want."

The pilot cut the engine down to half throttle as they approached the east bank of the river. "And how am I going to retrieve you? I have a hard enough time powering against this current. Swimming against it seems a bit beyond your capabilities."

Colin wasn't as spry as when Sanguine had dumped him in hell. Though only months had passed for her, it had been years for him. "They close the river walk past the ferry in about half an hour. There won't be anyone wandering around except some security guards, and your boat is small enough not to be detected so far below the wharf. Meet me just this side of the paddle wheeler. If you don't see me, work your way this direction until you're back at the mall. I should find what I'm looking for between those two landmarks."

The pilot looked over the course Colin had laid out. "That should work. Once you're in the water, I'll head back to port just to check in. No point hanging around looking conspicuous if I don't have to."

Colin nodded. The pilot cut the engine to idle and drifted the boat up to the waterlogged pilings. After checking the gear, Colin slipped off the back of the boat and into the cold water of the Mississippi.

The current bashed him into one of the wooden posts just as the pilot boat motored back into the channel. Colin took a pull at the oxygen mouthpiece before submerging himself in the black water filled with obstacles. Even with the waterproof flashlight, he could only see ten feet ahead due to the mud churned up by the river. *I must be out of my mind, thinking I'm going to find my safe in all this muck.*

In spite of his apprehension, he worked his way down to the river bottom and started his methodical search. The wooden pilings formed a grid pattern under Spanish Plaza. Being careful not to be swept past the next row of stripped tree trunks, he worked his way from the rapidly moving river to the shore under the raised cement floor of the plaza. River rats bigger than his head scurried along the muddy beach. They didn't appear to be afraid of him in the least.

"Find me my vault."

The rat nearest him sneered and carried on with his nightly vigil. *Damn it. I could really use some bigger creatures at my command right now.* Other than his squadron of mosquitoes, he couldn't be sure any life form would listen to him anymore.

He worked around the next support and dove back into the river. The closer he came to the end of the row of wooden beams, the harder the river pulled at him. Hanging onto the trusses kept him from being swept away but made the search that much harder. *No wonder the fail-safe dumped the vaults out here. No one in his right mind would be able to locate one.*

After twelve passages from beach to river and back, he

developed a routine. From each support, he scanned the area with his flashlight. His strength was failing, but he felt sure he hadn't bypassed his vault.

As he struggled back toward the shore, he cut his forehead on a corner of submerged metal. In spite of the pain, he ran his hands over the rectangular metal structure. *This is it. It has to be.*

Unfortunately, it was half-buried in the silt. He left his prize, returning to shore to catch a breather and consider what best to do with the massive box. Breathing air, even the creosote-laden mist kicked up by the waves, beat the purified oxygen from the tank. "It's too big to simply haul out of the river. I should have guessed that after spending so much time in Luther's vaults."

He looked at the rat, which stared at him as if he were some alien creature. "Guess I just thought he wouldn't waste so much space on a handful of objects. He must have been expecting Kendell to dig up a lot more of my old junk."

The rat squeaked and hurried off after some unseen prey.

"Right. What's inside isn't the problem at hand. If I open it underwater, I could dig out what I want, but the current might sweep my stuff out into the river." He looked around at the short overhang. He barely had room to sit. "This space is too small to stand it upright, but I might be able to prop the door far enough open to squeeze inside." He shook his head as the thought of being trapped in the underwater crypt elicited nightmares of past horror stories. "Damn you, Luther Noire."

He thought back to what he remembered about the

vaults in the World Trade Center. *The doors are sealed so tightly that nothing could escape. So that box must be airtight. Assuming I can get it free of the mud, it should float. If I can't bring it ashore, I'd need to get it out into the river.*

The riverbank was littered with debris ranging from red plastic cups to shipping blocks and tackle. But before he began rounding up tools, the image of being stuck in the vault lined up with his memories of Luther's building. *Those vaults aren't just airtight—they're cut off from the outside dimension. If I could drag that safe somewhere unnoticed by Sanguine, it might prove useful. Even though it wouldn't give me access to other realms, it would make me undetectable in this one.*

He searched for the longest, heaviest rope he could find. A light struck him in the face, temporarily blinding him. Once it moved off down the shoreline, he made out the blue pilot boat. *Damn. I must have been down here longer than I thought.* He used his flashlight to signal the boat.

To relieve himself of an additional swim through the current, he secured the rope to a hook on the vault then dragged the end with him as he worked his way out of the comparative safety of the wharf. He held on tightly to the last wooden support as the pilot boat drifted in closer than Colin found comfortable.

"Find what you were looking for?" the pilot asked.

"Yep, but it's buried in the silt. It's also larger than I remembered." He held up the line. "Think your boat could tug it off the river bottom?"

"This boat may look small, but she's got a lot of power. If you can free it from the mud, I can haul it out." He took the end of the rope and secured it to a cleat on the side of the boat. "Just make it fast. My friend across the river isn't going to wait all night."

"Once we get it free and floated downriver, I'll have you drop me and the vault off past the shipping docks," Colin said. "After that, I'll give you this gear to take back to your friend."

"Just make sure there's another five hundred in the pockets."

*Greedy bastard.* "You and your friend will get paid. I don't imagine you've got a shovel up there, do you? Or do I have to pay a surcharge for any equipment used from the boat?"

The pilot smiled. "We're an all-inclusive operation." He dug around under the visitor's seat and pulled out a folding emergency spade. "Don't take too long. I feel like I'm showing my ass out here—and there aren't any Mardi Gras beads headed my way."

"I suppose the difference between flashing and public indecency is mostly a matter of the season." Colin ducked back below the water line and pulled at the rope to get back to the vault.

As if the water weren't murky enough, as he dug at the silt, it turned into an opaque cloud of greenish brown only visible in the light from the pilot boat. Colin resorted to using one hand to gauge the confining mud while using the shovel in the other to clear the vault. He could practically hear the boat pilot demanding that he move faster. Once he felt the vault give at the other end of the rope, he swam back to the surface. "Give it a tug. If it comes loose, I'll stay down here to guide it past the piers."

Halfway back to the vault, Colin's legs started to cramp.

He didn't need the reminder that he was a businessman and not a world-class swimmer. His forehead was still bleeding from his initial run-in with the vault, and he had trouble knowing which way was up in the swirling water. The rope lurched in his hand, the only warning of the pilot hitting the gas and pulling the vault free from the river bottom.

In spite of his intention to guide the vault out of its confinement, Colin found he had to hold onto the rope for dear life as he was pulled from the relatively calm water under the wharf to the unforgiving chaos of the Mississippi River. A series of hard jerks of the line indicated the vault had encountered the line of wooden posts between it and the open water. Each time the line lurched in his hands, Colin felt as if he were grasping the handhold of a bucking steer. *I'm no swimmer, and I'm no cowboy. If I get out of this, I'm never again going to complain about spending my workdays behind a desk.*

When the vault finally stopped resisting its liberation, Colin spun in the conflicting currents and eddies of the river with only the rope as his lifeline. Even the bubbles from his regulator seemed lost as to the surface of the water. He couldn't remember ever being more at the mercy of another human being.

The rope swung in a lazy arc, moving from the direction of the river flow to perpendicular to the force. When it swung again so that Colin had to hang on, he knew they were close to docking.

As if someone had turned off a fire hose, the rush of water stopped. The rope in his grasp pulled him toward the surface of the water. He broke out of the confining river back into the dark of night and saw his treasured vault floating behind him. Beyond the vessel, the concrete jetty held a peaceful backwater lagoon that the boat had swung into.

Like a fish on the line, Colin felt the pilot pulling on the rope to get him back to the boat. In the dive equipment, he lost track of the hull until his head bumped into the solid metal side. He tightly grasped the lifeline as the pilot hoisted him out of the water. In the heavy slippery gear, he flopped onto the deck.

"You must be the craziest son of a bitch I've ever met. Never heard of anyone shooting the river underwater like that."

Colin pulled off the oxygen mouthpiece, wondering how he hadn't bit it in two. "Glad to have provided some entertainment."

# 5

*S*anguine was in for a fight with Kendell, but there was no point delaying the inevitable. Waiting around until dusk for their usual meeting would just be a waste of Sanguine's time, and she needed to get back to watching over Colin. She hitched up her wings and walked into Scratch and Sniff. Cardboard-cutout Delphine looked away from her customers and nodded toward the back room.

"I shouldn't be long," Sanguine said. "But you might want to shut the door just the same. There might be yelling."

The flash across Delphine's eyes was enough of an indication that the real voodoo practitioner had checked in. "Try not to break anything."

"I can't make any promises." Sanguine tried not to be too judgmental of the hidden voodoo library as she squeezed into the small space. The fact that the library was located in a secret closet, however, made her think the voodoo

79

priestess was still trying to hide her passion. Sanguine took a seat in the guest chair. The walls were lined with bookshelves filled with hundred-year-old ledgers that gave the room a feeling of voodoo oppression.

Kendell's seventh-gate voodoo totem, with attached golden guitar pick, sat on a small table. Sanguine turned the totem toward her. *This must be the dumbest form of communication ever.* She rapped on the totem's head as if trying to wake the spirit inside. The action was completely unnecessary. Seeing Delphine out front was all that Sanguine had needed. The voodoo practitioner was responsible for notifying Kendell.

Like a three-dimensional hologram, Kendell appeared in Delphine's African-motif throne. "You had me worried. How did your meeting with Colin go?"

"I told you I might not be able to check in every day. Keeping out of sight does make it tricky, you know."

Kendell sat back against the gold fabric. "When you get defensive this quickly, I know we're in trouble."

Sanguine wondered if she should take up playing cards with the gamblers on the riverboat in order to develop a poker face. As things stood, Kendell had too many ways of reading her.

"I slept with him. And before you get all fussy with me, I used another body. But I'm pretty sure he knew it was me."

From the way Kendell squirmed in the towering chair, Sanguine knew her friend wanted to chastise her as if she were a high school slut.

"I can see why you'd want some time to yourself after

something like that," Kendell said. "So he knows he's in hell?"

"I think he knows we're playing a game with him, but that doesn't necessarily mean he thinks he's in hell. He'd have to assume that, since we built one alternate dimension, another was also possible. He's as cagey as always about revealing too much. If he does think he's in hell, he doesn't seem to be in a hurry to break out."

Kendell crossed her legs and shook her foot at Sanguine. "You're giving him a reason to stay. Though I can see the short-term benefit—especially to me—in the long run, your play will only make it more difficult to contain him. He'll get to know you just as much as you're getting to know him. I know from experience how good he is at discovering an opponent's weaknesses. And if he does develop feelings for you, once you leave hell, he'll have double the reason for trying to break out."

*That's assuming he still wants you.* Sanguine resisted the urge to get into a catfight over someone they both supposedly despised. "One step at a time. I need to figure out what he's up to. That means getting close."

Kendell stopped fidgeting. "So you're going to sleep with him again?"

"He never seemed the type to accept the friend zone. If I want information from him, I'm going to have to be less aloof. I'm keeping him dangling on whether this relationship continues, but once the sex card is played, it's not easy to put it back in the hand."

Kendell leaned forward. "Please tell me you're not considering coming out of the shadows. You were the one who said Colin needed to figure out he was in hell all on his own. One look at those wings, and we'll have the ruthless devil pounding on the walls of hell again. Even with Luther in charge of the World Trade Center, I'm not sure we'll be able to contain Colin a second time. He learns from his failures."

"Don't be stupid. I can keep using that little plaything sex-bot for the time being. If he does figure out our game, though, I am going to have to physically confront him. The longer we have this psychic sex, the harder it's going to be to cut it off when we do meet for real." Just saying the words that she would likely let Colin fuck her angelic body made Sanguine shiver with both fear and anticipation.

Kendell nodded as if Sanguine had asked permission. "Are you finding anything useful about him?"

"Do you mean some weakness, or something redeemable?"

Kendell wasn't making eye contact. "I'd like to say either would be helpful, but the truth is, I don't want you falling in love with the devil. I'm well aware of how charming he can be, but it's just a game to him."

Sanguine wondered if they hadn't played their game a little too well. Kendell, the sexy bait that was used to entice Colin into this new hell, was never presented as a potential partner for him, only a desired prize dangled in front of him like raw meat before an alligator. He couldn't really be faulted for acting on his male urges.

"I'm not trying to trick him. To find out what he's thinking, he'll need to trust me. Teaching him to jump through hoops like an ill-behaved dog going through obedience training isn't working so well."

Kendell gripped the lion-head ends of the chair arms. "That was not the intention of the seven gates, and you know it."

"Well, they weren't meant to let him back into life. Tell me, what exactly was your plan if he showed he'd changed? Once you set up the rules, you're as much responsible for playing by them as he is."

"He's never going to change," Kendell said.

*You're my friend, but you are a fool.* "Maybe that's what I'm trying to find out. Miss Fleur told me about the Archibald she remembered. I can't say he treated her as I'd want a partner to treat me, but he wasn't the definition of evil that he is now. According to her, that cane changed him. What if, now that he's no longer under its influence, he returns to being an average though ambitious businessman?"

Kendell finally looked at Sanguine's eyes. She stared into her as if trying to delve into her soul. "You met with Fleurentine?"

"I needed someone to talk to after sleeping with Colin. You were just going to fight with me."

Kendell uncrossed her legs and hunched down in the chair like a scared little girl. "It's not that. You went to the convent. How can you be sure Colin didn't see you?"

Sanguine became infected with Kendell's fear. "You think he figured out his long-dead wife is the guardian of the third gate?"

"I think you might have just shown him the way. I guess

that locks you into your current course of action. We need to learn what he knows."

~

As KENDELL LEFT Delphine's shop, she kicked herself for being so inattentive to what Sanguine was going through. As the only guy in hell, Colin represented a challenge to the phrase *I wouldn't sleep with you if you were the last man on earth.* The truth was, if Kendell hadn't had Myles as her rock, she might have given in to the temptation as well.

She wandered back to the apartment, wondering how she was going to explain this latest development to Myles. He didn't have a hang-up about sex, but he did have one about Colin. In hell, her doppelgänger was walking the same street. She stopped at the corner and turned toward the river. Confronting Colin wasn't part of the plan. He needed to figure things out on his own, not have her go blabbing out questions about his intentions toward Sanguine. Besides, any interaction with Kendell could too easily turn his attention from staying in hell to again trying to break down the walls between the dimensions.

*No. I need to go home and feed the dogs then get to the club. Acting without thinking about the consequences has gotten me into enough trouble. Hopefully, Sanguine and Colin will show up at the gig tonight so I can see their chemistry. Right now, that's the best I can do.*

She turned back to her and Myles's apartment with a feeling of calm. Sanguine was a big girl. She didn't need Kendell telling her what to do or judging her sex life.

The moment Kendell opened the door, Cheesecake jumped off the ottoman and came running. Doughnut Hole wasn't far behind.

"Hey, guys. Where's Myles? Is he already at the club?"

The two dogs danced around her for attention.

She got down on the floor to play with the pups. "Just between us, I'm beginning to think that Papa Ghede gave us that club just to keep us out of trouble. What do you think?"

Cheesecake let out a definitive bark of agreement.

"I'd better get changed and hustle over to the club, but first, let's get you two some dinner."

The dogs played around her, distracting her from her obligations. "You two would have me sit here and give you love all day, every day. And I would if I could. But there's a world to save."

She picked them up one at a time and gave them big snuggles before heading to the kitchen for their food. Once she'd seen to it that they didn't get into a fight over the last morsels of kibble, she adjourned to the bedroom to change into her fishnets and short skirt. The outfit wasn't the sexiest in her repertoire, but it was close. She could use the excuse that she wanted to entice Myles—which was never a lie—but if Colin was present, she really wanted to gauge his interest in her. There was no use worrying unduly about Sanguine if Kendell was still his primary lust.

She grabbed her guitar case and headed out the door but not before giving the dogs one last head rub for good luck.

$\approx$

MYLES DID his best to keep calm while Kendell explained why Sanguine had slept with Colin. Intellectually, he knew she was right. Sanguine was more than capable of taking care of herself. But emotionally, he really wanted to punch Colin in the jaw.

With Charlie getting the bar ready and the band setting up onstage, it wasn't the time or place to get into a heated discussion with Kendell. Not that anything was her fault, but women had a way of defending each other—even if that meant Colin got off without the justice he deserved.

"What do you propose we do?" he asked.

"I can't keep as close an eye on him as I'd like while I'm playing onstage. Watch for him getting into a conversation with a woman. Either he'll be looking for another hookup, which means very few words and a quick hustle out the door, or he'll be on the prowl for Sanguine. From what we witnessed last time, and the fact they recently had sex, if you see the two of them talking, it'll be a more emotional exchange than anything he's gotten into before."

Myles remembered all too well how Sanguine had put Colin in his place. The last thing he'd expected was for them to wind up in bed together. "Can you please stop referring to them having sex? The image is just disturbing."

"Sanguine wasn't using her body. Think of it more like some virtual-reality game."

He gave her the side-eye. "That's not helping."

"I know you see her as a kid sister. I guess that's inevitable after protecting her comatose body on our couch for so long. She is hell's angel, though. No one has a better handle on that realm than Sanguine. She'll be safe."

Myles never did understand women. They could be so focused on the emotional side of things one minute and totally concerned about physical safety the next. "I'm not worried about her picking up some Wiccan STD. Colin's a manipulative bastard. I know Sanguine isn't a virgin, but I can't imagine she's ever dealt with a man so cunning before. Baron Malveaux used sex like a knife to cut away a woman's sense of self. There are more ways of getting hurt than just physically."

Kendell reached across the bar to hold his hand. "You really are one of the good ones."

Though he always appreciated her compliments, they had a way of softening him up for some request that wasn't in his nature. "If I do see him talking to a woman instead of just hauling her out the door, what do you want me to do —follow them?"

"Sanguine will still be undercover. We don't want to give away her identity. If you go all protective older brother, Colin will know something's up. Sanguine has been very clear that he needs to figure out his situation on his own. I need to make sure she's in charge. If our hypothetical woman looks like she's being overly flirtatious, we'll know we've got a problem."

Myles had real trouble envisioning Sanguine as flirtatious. "So in other words, if she doesn't haul off and punch him in the face?"

Kendell gave him the look that said, *Don't be an ass.* "She's trying to get closer to him. I expect them to carry on some form of conversation and probably leave together. Knowing Colin, you can expect a certain amount of touching. I just don't want her initiating anything sexual."

Once Kendell headed back to the stage, Myles settled into his usual bartending routine. As always, he lost track of the night as the band started getting into its set. Slinging bottles with Charlie had become so well choreographed that they often finished each other's drinks. But when his double in hell spotted Colin entering the club, Myles dropped a bottle of tequila. "Damn it."

Charlie tossed a couple of rags on the floor. "Don't worry about it, Boss. Not like it was a top-shelf drink."

"It's not that. I just spotted someone I'd just as soon not have to deal with enter."

Charlie made a quick survey of the room. "You need a minute out back?"

"Not this time. I need to see what he's up to. I kind of doubt he's here to talk with me tonight. Let's keep the show simple, though. I'd rather not be known as the clumsy bartender."

Charlie made quick work of the replacement margarita. "No worries. Just give me a heads-up if you intend on getting into a paranormal fistfight. Not that there's much I can do to break up an interdimensional brawl, but you're going to look pretty silly air punching."

"Very funny."

Myles let muscle memory carry him through the mixologist routine while listening in on conversations in two dimensions. For the most part, the participants matched up with their unknown cardboard-cutout doubles. The trick was to watch for a woman who acted differently in hell, especially if she was in Colin's proximity.

"Rum and Coke."

Myles heard the words but didn't see the customer until he consulted hell's dimension. "Coming right up." He refrained from engaging Colin in anything more than a professional interaction.

"Did you happen to notice that long-legged blonde I left with the other night? I was hoping to continue our conversation."

*I'll bet you didn't even catch her name.* "She usually rolls in about eleven. Here's your drink." He smiled at his restraint at not tossing the rum and Coke in Colin's face.

When the devil left, Myles looked at Kendell rocking out to "Cherry Bomb." She graced him with a smile—a reward for not going off script with Colin.

A short redhead with so many freckles Myles suspected she'd spent the weekend tubing on the river leaned back against the bar and spoke to him over her shoulder. "Back off. You're cramping my style."

From the fact that the same woman in life was dancing so close to her date that their clothes were bunching up, he knew his interdimensional visitor had to be Sanguine. "Just keeping an eye out for you."

"More like keeping an eye *on* me. I can just imagine the spin Kendell put on my plan while she was explaining it to you. I can take care of myself, you know."

Myles knew her fierce independence came from relying on herself for most of her life. She'd probably never had anyone express as much concern as he and Kendell had.

"That was never in doubt, at least not from me. I've seen you in action, but someone watching your back is never a bad idea."

She finally turned to him. "I know, and I do appreciate your concern. Just don't interpret everything Kendell says as me being a foolish child, okay?"

"Deal. Looks like your avatar just walked in. If you don't want to have to explain why she's about to give Colin the cold shoulder, you'd better get to work."

The redhead returned to the dance floor to mirror the moves of her reality counterpart as the blonde deviated toward Colin. Myles tried to remain attentive while appearing uninterested as the two took up their game of sexual cat and mouse.

Watching Sanguine flirt with the devil was like watching a kid sister on a stripper pole. Somebody was bound to get hurt, and the odds were against her. *She can take care of herself.* He only hoped the rationalization for his remaining behind the bar held true.

If she'd requested a drink, Colin didn't oblige. Sanguine probably didn't want to risk a confrontation between the two men, but Myles would have preferred to have her and Colin close enough to pick up on their discussion. For twenty frustrating minutes, they played their game of seduction. When they did leave, Myles couldn't tell who'd initiated the progression from noisy club to quiet seclusion. He considered following after them like a jilted lover, but Kendell was right. That kind of behavior would only tip Colin off about Sanguine's true identity.

He checked his watch but not to see the time. After a

quick bit of math, he came up with Sanguine having a little more than four months before she would voluntarily accept rescue from hell. *I've had relationships that lasted less time than that.*

He returned his marionette to autopilot and looked at Kendell onstage. She graced him with a quick smile meant only for him before refocusing on her part of "Barracuda." Hell might beckon, but life was certainly sweet.

THE NIGHT WAS SO LOVELY that Kendell and Myles didn't head straight home after the gig but turned toward the river. She had grown to rely on his counsel when it came to dealing with the paranormal. He wasn't always right, and she still had to take charge, but he saw things in less emotional terms than she did.

Even strolling in the beautiful fall night, she couldn't prevent her fears for Sanguine from dominating the conversation. "We're going to need a plan for getting Sanguine out of hell. I know I said I'd give her six months, but if she intends on moving this relationship from having multiple one-night stands to being lovers, we're going to have to step in." Paper silhouettes of skeletons and witches hung in the windows of the homes in the Marigny, adding to the Halloween spirit.

"I wondered how much freedom you were going to allow her."

"I'm not freaked out about the sex part," Kendell said. "Honestly, I don't even think I'm afraid of her falling in love, though if she did, I'd need to slap some sense into her. If he falls for her, though, I don't see how she'll be able to leave. Don't you think she's going to make him even more motivated to escape hell once we get her home?"

They walked up the concrete steps to the levee. He stared out at the water for so long she feared he hadn't heard her until he said, "She's at home in hell."

"What are you talking about? We're her home." Kendell wanted to scream. "I know she digs flying around with those angel wings and being able to see the future—which, by the way, I'm not sure I believe. For an oracle, she blunders an awful lot. But she can't possibly be content with Colin as her only actual companion."

He took her outburst in stride. "I'm just telling you what I see. She was miserable when she woke up in life. She didn't have a purpose, and all we could offer her was a job as shot girl at the club. Would you really give up being a guardian angel to pour drinks down frat boys' throats?"

She stared out at the river, hoping the lapping water would calm her emotions. "Do you know how much I hate it when you're right?"

"I promise not to tell," he said. "You're not wrong about needing to do something about Sanguine, though. I just don't know what that would be. We promised her six months, but I share your concern that she'll be too entrenched in that reality to leave. And I don't just mean because of her feelings for Colin."

Kendell pulled her coat around her and sat on the metal bench to watch the water. "You once said you wouldn't give me up to Colin even if it meant he'd no longer be the devil. Does that hold true for Sanguine as well?"

He sat so close she could feel his warmth through her thick coat. "What if we turned that idea on its head? If Colin stopped being the devil in order to get Sanguine back, would we let him back into life?"

Kendell thought she'd have punched anyone else who had come up with that idea, but she trusted Myles enough to explore it. "You mean encourage him to work through the seven gates? Sanguine thought he might try, but she said he'd only do it as a challenge to her."

"As you just pointed out, her vision of the future doesn't always come with explanations. What if he is bettering himself because of her but not because he's trying to outmaneuver her? Women have a way of healing even the worst men with their love. Isn't that why you keep giving Colin the benefit of the doubt?"

She felt a cold shiver cross her arms and back. "My interest in him was never romantic. I saw right through his suave advances. I just thought he hadn't gotten a fair hearing." She held tightly to Myles's hand. "You don't ever need to worry about me being interested in someone else."

He leaned in and kissed her on the cheek. "I know. But I also know women have a need to rescue the man drowning in his mistakes. Take me, for example. When we met, I was lost in self-doubt. You gave me a direction. Colin has built walls of greed and self-importance that are stronger than the hell you and Sanguine have him confined in. To a woman who thinks she's an angel, that might be a challenge worth taking."

"She has a way of covering up her heart with snarky banter. She attacks so she doesn't have to expose her weaknesses. Once she told me that the more difficult she is with someone, the more she likes them."

"Hatred and love are sometimes two sides of the same emotional coin—though a person doesn't usually express them both at the same time. Dating Sanguine, with her mixture of emotions, must be like being caught in a summer thunderstorm—bright and sunny one moment, zapped by lightning the next."

Kendell had hoped Sanguine's intense dislike of Colin would prevent her from getting too attached, but if Myles was right, she might already be falling in love. "So you're saying either they're going to have sex for real, or she's going to kill him."

"Love hurts."

## 6

*S*anguine stood Annie's naked body in front of the full-length bathroom mirror. The girl was attractive enough but the type who looked better in clothes than out of them. In the tight-fitting party clothes that Sanguine had been forced to endure at the club, Annie looked thinner in places and more curvaceous in others than she actually was. Sanguine's own body was muscular to the point of being intimidating, but living in the swamp required more athleticism than being a college student.

She turned to inspect the ample rear end as if judging the lines of an automobile. *Definitely a sports car, but meant for the guy who wants the look more than the performance.*

The closet was meticulously organized. Jeans, oversized men's shirts, and sweat clothes took up the first third. *Weekend wear.* The college-class selection consisted of low-cut tops and snug-fitting pants. Sanguine could envision the body looking far more enticing with the pencil-leg stretch jeans dictating the curves of legs and butt. The final third of Annie's collection looked like outfits that belonged to a kid sister—short skirts, brash colors, and tops that didn't start buttoning until well past the cleavage.

*Have you seriously never been to an upscale restaurant?* Sanguine felt momentarily sorry for the girl. *It's no wonder Colin thought you wouldn't be able to carry on a conversation for more than five minutes. Give yourself more credit, girl.* Sanguine doubted Annie would get the message, but being in her body might at least leave some residual self-respect.

She closed the closet and walked naked into the roommate's bedroom. Though a fellow party girl, the woman at least had dresses that went below the thighs. Sanguine picked out a knee-length black dress that wouldn't cut off her ability to breathe.

She double-checked the overall effect in the mirror. Though it wasn't the best representation of how Sanguine would have dressed for a formal dinner, it beat the long, flowing goddess dress she'd been confined to with her wings. *Okay, Colin, let's get this game started.*

A town car was waiting for her when she exited the off-campus apartment. Colin stood out front as the attentive suitor. Though Sanguine occupied Annie's body, some of the girl's muscle movements came too naturally to resist. She did a seductive spin to show off her body as much as the dress.

"You're beautiful. Not that it was ever in any doubt, but that outfit makes you look far more sophisticated than the girl I met at the club." He opened the back door and offered his hand to help her in.

*I'm not infirm,* she thought. But she accepted the masculine gesture. "Glad I can still surprise you."

He joined her in the back and let the driver know they were comfortably ready to go. "Have you ever been to Commander's Palace?"

The game had begun. "I have not. Dating college boys usually means my dining choices top out at Bulldog Brewery, but I've heard wonderful things about the place."

He sat back against the black leather seat with a look of smug satisfaction.

*Score one for me. He thinks he'll be able to sweep me off my feet.*

"I've made the reservation for seven o'clock, so we have time for some cocktails before dinner. They have a lovely bar."

*I'll bet. I wonder how many of the women you've taken there never made it to the main course.* "I'm in your hands."

The smoldering look of desire in his eyes made her feel like a live chicken dangling on a string above an alligator. "I'll keep that in mind." He put his hand on her bare leg.

*Easy, big fella.* She covered his hand with hers to prevent any further advances. By squeezing his fingers, she hoped he'd realize who was actually in charge. "We have the night ahead of us. I've been looking forward to this dinner for some time."

He took his hand off her leg and worked his arm around her shoulders, but the look of desire didn't leave his eyes. "I like a woman who enjoys the game of seduction. I'm in no hurry."

Before she could respond, the town car pulled up to the

restaurant entrance. The maître d' opened her door before the car came to a full stop. "Welcome to Commander's Palace, my lady."

In spite of Sanguine's distaste for ostentatious displays of the upper class, she had to admit she felt a bit like a Disney princess. "Thank you." *Surely, there's something more I should say.*

Colin whisked her hand under his arm and escorted her into the restaurant as if he owned the place. She still had questions, and chief among them was whether he knew he was in hell. His actions could have been nothing more than a high-powered businessman accustomed to deferential treatment, or they could have been the arrogance of a devil in his hell. The two positions were hard to differentiate.

Instead of sitting at the bar—where she'd have the opportunity to engage the bartender or other patrons—he guided her to a dark corner table. A waiter was on them before she'd situated her purse and adjusted her dress. "What would the lady like?"

She wanted a straight whiskey, but losing her edge wasn't the best play. "I'd love a Sazerac." Though the drink was still highly alcoholic, she could nurse it sufficiently to give Colin the impression she was getting tipsy while still staying clearheaded.

"I'll have the same."

*Nicely played. I'll bet you match me sip for sip.* "So what shall we discuss tonight?" *Check to the dealer.*

"I'd love to hear about your day. I find I can learn a lot about a woman just from the way she describes the simplest of events."

Even she didn't want to know about how Annie's day went. A guy who sat attentively while a woman droned on and on was only biding his time until he could start acceptably ripping his date's clothing off. "I'd rather hear about your day. Before we headed back to your place the other night, you said you were considering a business venture. How did that turn out?"

He looked like the cat who'd swallowed the canary. "It's progressing. I had a major breakthrough a couple of nights ago. Things are falling into place."

*Very good. You haven't said a damn thing.* "I'll bet your adversaries never see your play coming until it's too late. Are you looking at another hostile takeover?"

"I said I was in acquisitions. You were the one who made the leap to ruthless corporate raider."

*You don't really think I'm that naïve.* "I stand corrected. But you haven't denied my observation about your competitors."

"I didn't get to this position of power by being predictable." He stared at her while taking a sip of his drink as if willing her to do the same. She obliged, to keep him from growing suspicious.

"Do you leave your adversaries anything when you're done? Or are you more the slash-and-burn type?"

He shrugged as if their plight wasn't his concern. "Depends on how they play the game. A worthy opponent isn't easy to find. It takes a confident businessman to leave another with the resources to rebuild. Taking them down to nothing is the easy play. I only crush those that have no business sitting at the table."

She couldn't help but wonder if he was referring to her. "And does that go for your love interests as well?"

He sat back as if she'd made an unforeseen move on the chessboard. "I'll confess there was a time when a woman who crossed my path had to proceed with caution. Women admitting they're the weaker sex only serves to bring out the aggressor in men. But then, I find confident women already know that. I'll bet not many of your boyfriends find their way into your bed uninvited."

*He's turned this around to be about me.* "Usually I'm pretty particular about my sexual partners. The other night with you wasn't my typical encounter."

"Do you regret it?"

*I'm not sure.* "Regret is for the vanquished."

"Sounds like something I would say."

The waiter came by to tell them their table was ready. She was certain the less populated dining room he guided them to was a nod to Colin's prestige, but she'd have been just as happy eating at the bar. Having Colin treat her like a Southern debutant wasn't a great way to get to know her date, but if letting him perform in his natural environment put him at ease, he just might let down his guard.

The waiter held the chair out for her as if she were so uncoordinated she might fall on her ass if she had to sit and scoot the chair on her own. In her mind, she could hear Kendell explaining that this was simply how things were done in fancy establishments. She smiled at the waiter as he left them to consider the menu in peace.

"So what were your impressions of our night together?" she asked Colin.

He took a larger drink of his Sazerac than she thought necessary. "You are a fascinating woman—perhaps the most interesting I've met in years." He took a bite of his foie gras. "You know, when I first tried this stuff, I couldn't stand it. The complexities of the tastes were lost on me. Only after I'd matured could I appreciate the nuances."

"Are you really comparing me to fattened duck livers?"

He smiled at her play. "I suppose I am. There was a time when I would have considered your bluntness a threat. These days I'm more drawn to women who aren't afraid of expressing themselves. Our night together made me rethink the women I've been with lately. I hate to admit it, but those one-night stands were pretty empty. I suppose that makes me a cad in your eyes."

"I'm not above a good night of passion for its own sake, but I usually get wined and dined before the event, not after."

He put down his fork and stared her in the eyes. "I never considered what we had as a one-time affair."

"I was only teasing you."

"Then you're open to a longer-term relationship?"

She wondered how long she could reasonably stretch out the beginning of their courtship. Getting information on his plans was constantly a matter of gathering clues and listening for what wasn't being said, and the better she knew him, the more easily she could hear the subtle distinctions. "I'm here with you now, and it would be rude to let you take me out to dinner then only reward you with a kiss good night. But I'm not willing to make any commitments beyond tomorrow morning."

A less creative man might have asked for the check, but Colin accepted the waiter's offered dessert menu. "You should try their espresso. It'll keep you up half the night."

~

AS WAS HER CUSTOM, Sanguine got out of bed as the sun crept over the horizon. Annie's body might not be the most athletic, but so long as Sanguine refrained from directing the activities with Colin, she had sufficient stamina. To keep him from making any further advances, she wrapped a luxurious bathrobe around her body and moved into the living room to enjoy the sunrise.

She stopped in a cold panic at the coffee table. Her hands shook as she picked up the pastel drawing of Serephine and Antoine Malveaux.

Colin's touch made her freeze. Based on his naked arms, which crept around her waist like boa constrictors, she assumed he hadn't bothered to cover up.

She waved the drawing over her shoulder in front of his face. "What's this?" Though she tried not to sound cross, the alarm that gripped her heart made her voice quiver.

"Those are my kids, or they were. Their mother drew that a long time ago. A friend recently found it in a trunk of my old belongings. It was from a different life."

*No shit. Kendell's going to freak out.* "Do you ever see them?"

"It's been a long time."

*Fuck. He must be figuring out the seven gates by now. But how can I be sure? I need to get out of here and consult with*

*Kendell.* "It must be hard being alienated from those you love."

He turned her toward him and untied the sash of the bathrobe. "People come and go in life. I've learned to be content with those that are close at hand."

She took hold of his arms and pushed him away from her body. "It's Monday morning. I've got class." She left it to him to figure out if she was talking about her education or personal refinement.

He let her go but stood facing her so she'd get a good look at his naked manhood. "Feel free to bring some clothes next time. If you don't have to run home to change each morning we're together, maybe one day I'll get to have breakfast with you."

*And by breakfast, you mean sex.* "I'll keep it in mind." Annie's preference for sparse undergarments worked in Sanguine's favor. She was dressed and out the door before Colin had prepared enough coffee to once again entice her to stay.

She ran far enough into the Quarter to be out of sight of Colin's loft. She couldn't talk to Kendell over the gate to hell without flying in from the bayou, and part of the deal with borrowing a body was returning it to where it belonged. Colin undoubtedly would have offered his town car, but that would have meant fending him off throughout the ride.

She hopped into the first available pedicab. "I need to get to Tulane as fast as possible. There's a ten-dollar tip in it if you can make it in under fifteen minutes."

∽

SANGUINE KNEW her body and dress were looking a little rumpled from lack of use. She needed a good flight to clear the mental cobwebs and fluff up her feathers, but there wasn't time. Plus, she wanted to *see* the future, not travel into it. Her two gators continued to stand watch under the oak tree along Bayou Saint John.

Left looked up at her as if expecting some kind of treat.

"I need to figure out what Colin is up to, but I can't see his future unless I'm observing him with these eyes. Even then, it's like watching a billiard ball bouncing off the sides of a pool table with me being the cue ball that initiates the action. If I deal with him just right, I might make him land in the pocket, but do it wrong, and he'll mess up all the other balls on the table. And I can't see beyond the first ricochet off the side bumper without following him into his future."

Left snapped at her and went back to watching the water.

"There is that. If I put too much force into the shot, he'll just go bouncing right off the table. I can't be responsible for making him try to break back into life."

No matter how she looked at the problem, the only way to see into his future was to expose herself as hell's angel. She looked down at her reptilian guardians, wishing she were as worry free as they were. "Stay here. I've got to go check in with Kendell. I only wish I knew if Colin going through the third gate was a good thing or a bad thing. I suppose since he's not trying to pursue Kendell by breaking down the walls of hell, I'll have to take any action of his as progress."

She slipped off the limb and spread her wings for the short flight to the edge of the Quarter. Every flap was filled with dread. She dragged her feathers into Delphine's shop and sat in front of the voodoo totem like a little girl called to the principal's office.

Kendell looked far too happy as she materialized on the other side. "It's so good to see you, but you look like hell."

Sanguine pulled her wing around and saw the dirt caked into the feathers. "I suppose I do. Too much time sitting in the trees. I guess I'll have to check in with the birds to figure out how they stay so clean."

"Just don't go swimming naked in some angel-sized birdbath."

She laughed in spite herself. "I've got news, but I can't figure out if it's good or bad. Colin has made it through the third gate."

Kendell's look of merriment switched to concern. "Are you sure?"

"I saw the drawing from Miss Fleur. Has anyone on your side thought to check in with her?"

Kendell closed her eyes tight. "That would have made sense, wouldn't it? No. I haven't checked in on her. I guess that will be my next stop, followed by checking on Baron Malveaux's children at the fourth gate."

"Go easy approaching the nuns. They might be getting a little testy about us using their convent as a meeting hall. Honestly, I'm still not sure Colin knows he's in hell. The convent is an embassy in both of our dimensions, so he could have checked in on her from either side. He didn't try to hide the drawing from me, and he didn't gloat about having it. After that first gate, he seems to be just stumbling through them as if they're opening all by themselves."

"The band didn't just let him pass," Kendell said. "But I know what you mean. We didn't exactly question him. Do you think he achieved some power over the gates when he broke into our ceremony?"

Sanguine wasn't the best at understanding men, but even Colin didn't seem that devious. "It's a possibility, but we won't know until you talk to Miss Fleur. I can't see how he would have gotten hold of the drawing if she hadn't given it to him, but if you were right about him seeing me leave the convent, we might finally find out if he knows he's in hell. If he followed me in after I left, he would have asked her about seeing an angel."

"And if he is developing a connection to humanity?"

A part of Sanguine hoped that was true even though it went against her original plan to destroy him. "Then we're all to blame—or take credit. Myles gave him the ability to feel empathy when he entered the baron's old totem. You gave him hope by telling him redemption was possible. And apparently, I'm showing him the way."

"You're causing him to feel the beginnings of love." Kendell had a way of giving guys too much emotional credit.

"I wouldn't go that far. I'm more of a challenge than the bimbos he takes out back of the club to satisfy his frustration while you play onstage. I think he likes the distraction of having to participate in a conversation before getting his rocks off."

Kendell gave Sanguine the snarky half-smile that said,

*You're intentionally being stupid.* "No guy, not even a rich one, takes a woman out to a fancy restaurant *after* they've had sex. He's falling for you."

*Are you jealous?* Sanguine resisted the urge to say it out loud. It wasn't that she didn't want to know, but asking the question might make Kendell fixate on the idea. Having her go down that rabbit hole wouldn't help anyone. "Love is a pretty advanced experience for someone who's spent two lifetimes cutting himself off from all of humanity."

"He only started the process of isolation. We finished it by casting him into hell."

"You mean, I finished it."

"We share the blame," Kendell said. "I know I've been overly hard on you for being the executioner, but I can't say I would have done anything differently. I just want you to be careful with your heart, Sanguine. Love involves mutual trust. He wouldn't be developing feelings beyond attraction if he didn't think they were being reciprocated."

*Is that how you rationalized his desire for you? Do you see his feelings for you as invalid because they were unrequited?* "Are you asking if my intentions toward the devil are honorable? Because I'll confess that I don't know. He's interesting, and not just in the repulsive way I expected. I don't know where this takes us, but I've still got months to figure that out."

KENDELL DIDN'T SEE a reason to bother Myles with another trip to the convent. The nuns would never let him enter. If she went there on her own, maybe the Reverend Mother would be a little less defensive.

By the time she got to the doors of the convent, she was convinced that letting her in would be only a formality. She knocked on the door so hard her knuckles hurt.

When the door opened farther than the sliver she was accustomed to, Kendell tried to push her way in. "I need to see Miss Fleur."

The Reverend Mother stood in the opening. Her stern countenance was more of a blockade than the solid wood doors. "This is not a social hall. We don't just let people onto our grounds whenever they like."

Kendell realized she'd taken the guardians for granted. "I didn't mean to be so forward, but this is important. I think Colin may be trying to work his way out of hell, and Miss Fleur might have accidentally helped him. I only need to talk to her for a minute to find out."

"Miss Fleur has fulfilled her commitment to you. She's part of the *deep waters* now."

Kendell didn't have time to rehash her knowledge of how time could be manipulated in the convent. "I understand that, but you have let me talk to her before. This is important."

"Isn't it always? I'm sorry, but if you haven't gotten what you want from that poor soul already, I'm afraid you'll have to find another patsy. This convent is now closed to the voodoo realm, and that goes for the hell dimension Agnes Delarosa created as well."

She'd never heard of an interdimensional embassy closing its gates. "You can't do that. We need you."

"Unless you intend on becoming a novice and taking your vows, there's nothing left to discuss. Miss Fleur's life is over, as is her afterlife. Traveling into a person's past messes with their minds. That poor woman died in a state of dementia. I won't bring her forward in time again only to add to her past suffering."

Kendell left the convent feeling dejected. The nun was right. Miss Fleur had suffered enough in life—and later in Guinee—without Kendell making things worse. If the woman had given Colin the pastel drawing, Kendell was in no position to judge her. *Maybe I should have taken Myles after all. He always knows how to relieve my self-condemnation.*

Instead of heading toward the bank, she walked down to the club, where Myles would be preparing the bar for the night's activities. With any luck, he could contact Baron Samedi without them having to gain access to the old bank office. Kendell had snuck into the bank before, but that had been with Delphine's help. Turning the night watchman into a zombie didn't seem like the kind of approach that would work twice.

Myles was busy organizing the mixes behind the bar. "What happened? You look like someone failed to acknowledge how cute Cheesecake was looking today. Please don't tell me Sanguine went into details about her night of passion with Colin."

"I wish it were only that creepy. Our devil is playing his games again. Apparently we were supposed to be in charge of warning the remaining gates. He's made it past Miss Fleur. The nuns took that as their excuse to close their doors to me. They say they're finished helping—as if they did anything more than letting us meet with Miss Fleur."

He left a gallon jug of sweet-and-sour mix on the bar. "Since I'm in charge of the fifth gate, Sanguine the sixth, and you the seventh, that leaves Antoine and Serephine in Baron Malveaux's bank office as the only gate we haven't checked."

"I'd like to avoid breaking into the bank. Is there any way you could raise Baron Samedi? Since he's watching over the Malveaux children, maybe he can get a message to them."

Myles avoided making eye contact, which was never a good sign. "The loas have been keeping their distance since our break-ins of Guinee."

"I guess I shouldn't be surprised. Papa Ghede and Baron Samedi both warned us what would happen if we got caught in their realm. Hopefully, they're just lying low to let the rumors of living people walking among the recently dead fade away. But that leaves us having to sneak into the bank."

"Maybe not." He motioned toward the office beside the bar. "You and I are business owners. Going to the bank with the excuse of looking for a loan should at least get us past the front tellers. From what I remember, no one's using that old office. It is the seventh gate to Guinee, so Baron Samedi would have to respond if one of us were to enter. I'll bring the cane just as an added incentive."

Though it had been his idea, Myles felt like a fraud sitting in the bank's reception room, waiting for a representative to lead them to the loan offices. "Maybe this wasn't such a good idea." He nodded toward the domed cameras. "Even if we were to escape our escort, security is going to have eyes on us every second. I'll bet they're already running our pictures through their identification database as we speak."

"Don't be so paranoid. They already know who we are. We've both got our personal accounts here as well as the business's. We're just two entrepreneurs looking for a little help to remodel the old club. Nothing in New Orleans could be more mundane."

*Good point. They're probably listening in as well.*

A young female executive in a suit that likely cost more than Myles's entire wardrobe came in and smiled. "Please come with me."

As they walked into the bank's inner sanctum, Myles wondered what new hell they were about to encounter. Hopefully, Baron Samedi had detected them entering the building and would somehow smooth the way to their meeting, but with the bank in the hands of Colin's family, they were in enemy territory.

She led them past numerous small offices where bankers were meeting with clients. The farther they went, the more upscale the look of both lender and customer. From within each office they passed, a bank executive would eye Myles with curiosity and suspicion.

Finally, the woman ushered them into a corner office with windows that looked out on the French Quarter.

"There must be a mistake," Kendell said. "We were just here about a loan."

The elderly woman behind the massive oak desk had

penetrating eyes. Myles recognized them immediately as being exactly like her son's. He'd seen her before, but he had only hazy memories of her because he hadn't been in control of his body at the time.

"You're the bank president. Something tells me you're not interested in our business proposal."

She motioned them to the chairs facing her desk. "I'm Margery Laroque, mother of Lincoln Laroque. But then, you already know that. What have you done with my son?"

Myles hadn't felt so out of touch with his body since Baron Malveaux had taken possession. He struggled to walk to the chair and sit without crumpling to the ground. For once, he used the old cane as originally intended. "We're not responsible for what happened to your son. That was all his doing."

"Let's cut the bullshit. You know where he is. As president of the bank and silent partner in Laroque Industries, you can see why my interest is more than personal. You can either answer my questions here, or we can go down the street to my brother's offices."

Myles had already spent enough time in the police station to know that Chief of Police Laroque had conflicting interests when it came to his nephew. Publicly, at least, he'd be forced to back his sister, and that would mean Myles and Kendell would be spending time in jail until the bank president was content with their answers.

"Where do you want us to start?" he asked.

"How about with why you're here. I've looked over your little club's finances. Though they suck, you wouldn't be coming to me hat in hand after the history Kendell's family has had borrowing money from this establishment."

Kendell was shivering in the chair next to him. "Then you know we share a common ancestor in Baron Malveaux."

"Illegitimate on your end," the woman sneered.

Kendell sat a little straighter at the insult. "I'm not sure even the courts at the time would have considered the offspring of rape the victim's fault."

Margery Laroque reminded Myles of a rattlesnake that had just drawn blood. She didn't so much regain her composure as reset for a second strike. "That was a long time ago, but my question remains: what do you want?"

Myles would have been happy to let the women duke it out, but again, he hoped to avoid drawing in the police. "I'll assume that you know as much as we do regarding the fate of your son, even if you don't know his location. If that's the case, then you'll also be familiar with this building's history. There's an office we'd like to see. It holds some answers to our current dilemma."

She stared at him as if trying to decide how much to admit. "Baron Malveaux's office is kept just as it was when he died."

"Now who's slinging bullshit?" Myles stood the cane in front of him. "I may have been relegated to the outskirts of my awareness, but I remember Baron Malveaux confronting you and reclaiming his office while he was in control of my body. He bested you, and that understanding of how to make you grovel remains within me." The fact that she didn't immediately strike at him the way she had

Kendell gave Myles a feeling he didn't fully understand. *I gave Colin empathy by entering his totem. Perhaps the baron did something similar by giving me aggression when he was in my body.*

"Fine. When my ancestor, the baron, returned to the living, he did run his affairs from that office, but we're talking semantics. It is still the baron's office."

*You can't even acknowledge that he was using my body.* "Are you going to let us enter the office or not? Because if the answer is no, you can sit here until the end of your days, wondering what happened to your son."

"*Colin* is not my son. I simply wanted to know if it was time to declare him dead so the bank can be free to liquidate his belongings."

*Motherly compassion at its Malveaux finest.*

Kendell leaned forward in her chair. "Oddly, we're looking for the same answer. If we could have just five minutes in that office alone, I'm sure we could give you the assurance you need."

The woman's laugh sounded like a hyena fighting for a piece of meat. "I'm not letting you in there *alone*. And your assurances won't mean much in a court of law. So far, I don't see anything that you have to offer as being useful to me. If you know where Colin is, tell me. For that information, I'll let you into the office but not alone. I want to be there in case you do discover some hidden treasure."

Myles wasn't any fonder of Margery than he was of her son. "Colin is in hell. There are two ways that he might be freed—escape or pardon. We're here to find out how far he's progressed along one of those paths. That's as much as we can tell you."

"If I was a betting woman," the bank president said, "I'd put my money on escape." She reached into her desk drawer and pulled out an old-fashioned skeleton key. The old lock probably wasn't much for protection, and Myles knew the key was mostly a formality. The true security would be the camera, guards, and paranormal spells—of both Colin and Baron Samedi's conjuring. "I'm only doing this out of curiosity. The next time you want a *loan,* make an appointment."

Myles walked beside Kendell and behind Margery Laroque, like a man being marched to the gallows. The woman had called Kendell's bluff about their having some proof that Colin would remain among the dead if they entered the old office. Alone, they might have been able to summon Baron Samedi. They needed to talk to him if they had any hope of reaching the baron's children. With Margery present, however, the voodoo loa wasn't likely to show himself. That didn't leave any options as far as Myles could see. They might as well be walking straight into the police station.

He leaned in to whisper to Kendell, "I've got nothing."

"Samedi won't let us down."

Myles gripped the silver skull headpiece of the cane as they entered the office, but as he feared, there was no grand voodoo gesture from the loa of the dead. After seeing the office in its full seventh-gate-to-Guinee glory, he found the dark wood-paneled walls disappointingly stagnant. Kendell ran her hand over the large desk, but even that didn't call forth Baron Samedi.

The bank president stood at the door with her arms crossed. She reminded Myles of a schoolteacher waiting at the chalkboard for a student to finish so she could tell them they'd failed. "I could have told you that your plan required a miracle. This old office is nothing more than a museum exhibit. It was almost worth the diversion just to see the despondent looks on your faces, but now I do have to get back to work."

## 7

*H*aving Annie stay at his condo for a second night was a major success. After seeing Sanguine in flight, Colin was convinced his sexual partner was really the angel in disguise. Though he wanted to get past the initial hide-and-seek courtship, her use of the fake name and body helped him maintain an emotional distance from the swamp-witch-turned-angel. The superficial aspects of their conversations had been less enlightening than he'd wished. She stuck to her carefully prepared script regarding any details of her life. The role of a college student didn't fit her, though. Her insights into human nature and relationships were far too mature for a girl still going home from parties with the first dude who paid her a sincere compliment. He'd made himself an expert at identifying the type of woman who didn't take much work to seduce. Annie was too much of a contradiction *not* to be Sanguine.

The baron side of Colin wanted to viciously ravage the

college student as payback for Sanguine playing her game of deception. But he held back. Colin knew he was being conned, but having her think she held the upper hand had its benefits. The giddy excitement of having made a strong move had tripped up more than one opponent.

With the emotional chess game on hold, he turned his attention to pushing at the edges of his reality. He almost felt bad about staring downriver, but Sanguine had her game, and he had his. Until she showed up in the flesh as the winged angel, she was keeping secrets from him—and not just about her true identity. If she wasn't going to provide answers about his situation, he had a right to find them on his own.

He picked up the drawing of his children. Fleurentine had a way of accentuating their eyes to make them look as if they were begging for something. The effect left him cold. He dropped the picture back onto the table. It landed next to the plastic guitar pick as if the two were magnetically connected.

The worker's uniform of jeans and a heavy cotton shirt grated against his skin, but for where he was headed, he would have stuck out like a ship owner in his usual business attire. Jogging down the stairs to the street added a layer of sweat to the clothing. Though he doubted he could hide from Sanguine, her human puppets that filled his world could be easily fooled. If she wasn't going to present her angelic self, he might as well capitalize on her lackeys' stupidity.

He felt out of place walking through the well-manicured park along the river. Families and couples were enjoying the breeze off the river and discussing their next culinary adventure. He tried to tune them out. Once the smooth concrete path switched to the well-worn wooden dock, his clothing helped him blend in with the longshoremen.

He pulled his collar up around his neck and hurried along the gated-off shipyards. *I should have brought a pack of cigarettes to complete the look and use as bribes. Though talking to one of the workers could too easily expose me.*

When the wharf's wooden boards no longer looked strong enough to support the trucks and forklifts that plied the area, he moved inland. He had walked the same path back to his condo, but that had been at night, and he'd been soaking wet and exhausted. In the light of day, he struggled to remember the landmarks back to the small calm section of river.

He stopped at an abandoned parking lot with a No Trespassing sign hooked to the chain across the entrance. During his night's stealth maneuvers, he'd avoided the roads. He still nursed splinters from sneaking along the wharf that had half fallen into the water.

Caution dictated that he keep moving past his destination. A direct approach with the dockworkers so close could tip someone off about his treasure. He kept walking along the gravel path until it turned to a weeded lot that occupied the corner between the Industrial Canal and the Mississippi River. A small grove of stick-figure trees stuck out of the murky water.

He skirted down the embankment to the dead tree trunks. With a quick look around, he convinced himself that he was unseen. In spite of the October chill, it was a relief to pull off the denim jeans and flannel shirt. In only his swimsuit, he carefully folded up his clothing and stashed it under a stone of the levee.

The cold water made his muscles tense. Without the oxygen tanks, he wouldn't have the time underwater that he'd had when he'd moved the vault, but at least this time he knew where it was. The heavy ship rope was still tied to the submerged twisted rebar of the busted-up dock. He dove under the concrete overhang and traced the rope until his hand struck the metal vault. With a firm tug, he confirmed it was still floating free of the muddy river bottom.

Earlier in the day, he'd studied the river's topography and history. For hundreds of years, the tight bend had been notorious for shipwrecks. Though most had been cleared, wrecks outside of the shipping channel had a way of lying half-submerged until some developer found a use for that section of riverbank.

He worked out from the concrete ledge and stared past the Industrial Canal. At high tide, the trees that grew along the edge of the Ninth Ward obscured the riverbank. He searched for the opposite corner and tried to estimate one hundred yards downriver. Three times, he conducted his visual inspection before he caught sight of a pinpoint reflection of light off the broken wheelhouse window. The old luxury craft had run aground half a century earlier. *That's a long way to drag a safe.*

He swam back to shore and fabricated three stick boats from the debris of the dead trees. In the calm water, it was an easy swim with them back to the vault. The first boat he aimed at the shore and shoved far enough out to be caught by the ripples along the river's edge. The next he guided straight to his destination, and the third he flung far enough out to be whipped around by the strength of the river.

He watched the three stick boats and tried to extrapolate how he would deal with the challenges they encountered. When the bundle of twigs that braved the open river broke open and scattered across the surface, he focused his attention on staying as close to the riverbank as possible. None of his experiments survived the trip across the convoluted mixture of currents that occupied the conflux of the two waterways, but a handful of sticks did get lodged among the trees on the other side. *Good enough.*

As with the wharf under Spanish Plaza, he found all manner of junk lodged tightly under the cement overhang beyond the vault. He chose a hand winch and a paddle that had been snapped in half as the most useful objects. *Hopefully, I'll do better than the poor sod who thought he could raft down the Mississippi like a modern-day Huck Finn.*

Overthinking a problem had a way of creating data paralysis. He put aside thoughts of drowning while strapped to the vault, untied the rope, and yanked the three-quarters-submerged iron closet out into the river.

Lying on top of the bobbing metal box while it tipped and lurched its way downriver made Colin feel like some fool trying to sneak his pirate chest out of Davy Jones's locker. Even with the paddle, he was completely at the mercy of the unpredictable river. Waves splashed across the surface of the vault, making it hard for him to hang on and impossible to see where he was going. Staying alive and in possession of the vault took all of his energy.

He only knew he'd reached the far side of the Industrial Canal when the vault hit a submerged log, causing him to slide off the top. Though the river's edge was not shallow, he was able to put his feet into the slippery mud and tug on the rope. With more willpower than strength, he coaxed his prize toward the silt-covered beach.

Once ashore, all he wanted to do was collapse on the grass and pass out, but there was still too much to do and not much time. Whatever girlish activity Sanguine had chosen for her after-sex deliberation wouldn't take all day. Women only needed hours to consider their first mistake. After that, the self-loathing of cheap sex passed much faster.

A twang of pain struck him. *My time with Sanguine hasn't been some tawdry one-night stand.* He pulled harder on the rope to quiet his foolishness.

The *River Duchess* had plowed so deeply into the soft river bottom that only the wheelhouse and cabin remained above the waterline. The foredeck, however, was merely awash with water. Colin walked along the waterlogged teak surface while the vault banged at the boat's bow. The river that had threatened to end his life lapped like a puppy at his ankles. *This will do.* He tied the rope to the winch and hooked it to the wheelhouse hatch. It took a good half hour of ratcheting the winch to hoist the metal box over the railing. He kept pulling until he had the ungainly addition to the boat safely inside the cabin.

He fell into the captain's chair, so out of breath he feared he was having a heart attack. Across the inlet, dockworkers were carrying on as if nothing had happened. Boats continued to ply the river. He'd succeeded undetected.

*Since when do you sit back and enjoy a victory before you're done?* He wrestled his way out of the beat-up wooden chair and turned his attention to the vault. Communication cables that had been ripped out of their connections hung limply from the top. The iron hatch had been sealed shut. The emergency wheel turned freely but to no avail. He yanked the main handle across the width of the door, but nothing released inside the walls. *Damn it. There must be an override on this thing somewhere.*

Nothing along the walls indicated that there was magical button he'd somehow missed. He inspected the wires. *If I were designing this thing, I'd use a computer connection to tell the vault it was safe to open, but Luther has an aversion to advanced technology.*

He looked closer at the damaged square plastic box with protruding electrodes at the end of the cable. *Clever. Those aren't connections—they're sensors. As the fail-safe required a blood sacrifice, I'll bet this works the same way. DNA would be even more secure than a fingerprint.*

Colin wondered if the box would open for the descendent of the artifacts' original owner—if not the man himself—or if Luther had arranged for the box to open only for him. "Just in case Luther built some microphone into you, I'm Colin Malveaux, resurrected spirit of Baron Malveaux—the rightful owner of your secrets. I'm also hell's devil, and this is my realm." The last comment was a bluff, but Colin would take any advantage he could get.

Finding a bleeding wound wasn't a challenge. He dripped blood into the box from a gash on his forearm until the sensors in the small plastic box were completely covered.

A bang so loud it shook the deck echoed from inside the chamber. The door swung open just enough to let Colin know he'd succeeded. *Now the real work begins.*

He walked into the vault and pulled the door closed behind him. A green light lit up the confining space. *This thing must have some form of emergency power. Good.* The shelves were filled with boxes of his old possessions that had been secured in place, but he only opened the one containing his smoking paraphernalia. The pipe tool still had blood on it from its latest victim.

"You have proven to be quite the little troublemaker." He stashed the tool in his pocket as his connection to the other cursed objects in the vault.

But it wasn't simply having his things back that made his heart race. Those items were merely part of the plan—the magical line that connected him to the golden guitar pick lure. Now all he had to do was wait for the fish.

∽

"I NEED to check in with Sanguine." Kendell didn't really want to leave the apartment, but Sanguine would need to have grounding conversations with a friend now that she was playing her dangerous game of seduction.

Myles set Doughnut Hole on the ottoman. "I'll go with you. We can pick up dinner on the way home."

"I thought you hated Delphine's shop."

"I do, but I could use a little more information about that

cane Papa Ghede left me. If anyone would have some kind of instruction manual, it would be Delphine."

Kendell held his hand. "It'll be nice to know you're in the next room. Just try not to piss her off. We still need her shop as the seventh gate."

"You don't need to remind me."

As they walked through the Quarter, Kendell smiled to see the Halloween decorations. "I wish Sanguine would make it home in time for Krewe of Boo. She wouldn't even have to hide her wings."

"With every report from her, I feel like she's slipping farther away. Do you think she intends on honoring her six-month time limit?"

In spite of Sanguine's assurances that she would return home, Kendell feared the girl would be unable to control her emotional connection to Colin. Love had a strange way of spinning people onto foreseen destinies. "I'll subtly remind her. As much as I want her home, these last few months with you and no paranormal interference have been all I ever dreamed they'd be."

He let go of her hand to wrap his arms around her waist and pull her close. "I expect some magical piano to fall out of the sky at any minute to shake up our world again, so I'll take every minute of this normal life that I can get. Still, I'd go back to shouldering our part of saving the world if it meant having Sanguine home again."

"I hate feeling so useless. It's like I'm an injured volleyball player sitting on the bench, kibitzing each play. Sanguine doesn't need my meddling, but I don't know what else to do."

He kept an arm around her as they resumed their walk. "She knows we're here for her. Sometimes that's the best you can do for someone who's in danger. You rushing into hell would only add one more stress for her."

She couldn't stop the nagging feeling that Sanguine was growing too attached to Colin and needed a friend to help her see things straight. "At least I don't think she slept with him last night. I keep fearing she's going to go into details about their nights of passion."

Myles opened the door to Scratch and Sniff for her. "If she does, do me a favor and keep that conversation to yourself."

She left him in the front room of the establishment to consult with Delphine. Even though Kendell spent a great deal of time in the side room, staring at the voodoo totem in hell's realm, the connection never got any easier.

The sight of Sanguine sitting opposite her made the journey worthwhile. Sanguine's angelic smile, however, lasted for only a moment. Kendell's vision went hazy as she saw Sanguine reach toward her. The woman's scream faded as if a volume knob on the connection had been turned off.

The chair under Kendell dissipated, causing her to fall backward and land hard against a metal floor. Blackness covered her sight as if a blanket had been thrown over her head. She managed to bolt to her feet, but her senses weren't fully registering.

She wondered if she'd fallen into a dream state. "Where the hell am I?" The cold metal walls made her wrap her arms around her stomach.

"Give it a minute. Transitioning realms that abruptly can be disorienting."

She instantly recognized Colin's voice.

"What have you done?"

"I snagged your spirit out of the psychic communication you were having with Sanguine." His smug satisfaction caused her to ball her fists.

Her eyes began to clear. The metal closet she was in was lined with shelves and the same boxes she'd seen in Luther's office. She'd have to watch what she said in order to back whatever play Sanguine had going. "How?"

He reached into his pocket and pulled out the pipe tool that had started her adventure into the world of voodoo curses. "Simple really. You deposited your connection to the curse in the voodoo golden guitar pick. Everything you see around you, like this silly little pipe tool, represents my side of the curse. Luther's isolation box creates its own dimension, and my soul worked like the fly reel to pull you in."

*But what dimension do you think is outside this box?* Even asking the question, though, might hint that he wasn't back among the living. "Why?"

"Are we really going to go down the list of obvious questions? I want my cane back. Your boyfriend has it. I'm going to trade your spirit for my walking stick."

Her head began to clear. "So this isn't about continuing our conversation?"

"As much as I'd like to lie to you and say it was, this time I'm too busy for a chitchat. Right now, I suspect Sanguine is yelling her head off about you going into a mystical trance.

Delphine and your boyfriend will be freaking out. I could leave you here in my little trap and wander down to Delphine's shop, but I'm not sure what I'd find."

*He suspects, but he doesn't know.* "What do you mean?"

"Presumably, I'd see you lying in repose amid a flurry of activity. Being the natural suspect, I'd be immediately incarcerated in some fashion—probably in another one of Delphine's little statues. That wouldn't be an ideal situation for either of us as every minute they spend attacking me is a minute you'll be stuck in my dungeon."

She tried to remain calm. "I assume you have an alternative plan."

"I want to deal directly with Sanguine. She can be our intermediator."

*So that's what you're up to. You want to draw her into the open.* "What makes you think she would help you?"

"If it was simply up to her, I don't expect she would. But she'll work with the living and the damned to free you."

The room felt uncomfortably small with Colin standing in front of the closed hatch. "I can't do much stuck in your prison."

"I don't need you to do anything other than stay in this box," he said.

"How do you even know about our conversations? Have you been eavesdropping on us like some pervert?"

He motioned to all of the treasure chests stacked on the shelves. "I only came by this magic box recently. Like a hunter hiding in his blind, I had no idea how long I'd have to sit here until you accessed that voodoo totem." He held up the pipe tool. "I've been carrying this around as my little beeper should you power up the totem. Mind telling me why you had to use it to talk to your friend? She wouldn't happen to be trapped in another dimension again, would she?"

Kendell leaned back against the wall and folded her arms across her stomach. "If you want us to put our cards on the table, you start."

"Very well. I suppose these opening gambits have gone on long enough. Over the last few weeks, I've worked through a number of scenarios, ranging from me having returned to life to me being stuck in a virtual-reality totem. The most likely answer is that I'm still in that swamp witch's hell. Though how you two managed to make it look so much like life is a mystery. I know I've talked with you in this realm, but there are times you didn't seem quite real. Sanguine has been the bigger mystery. It's as if she can possess anyone she likes in order to play her games on me. Other than you two, I can't say for sure if I've met another real person. Most of the people I've interacted with are surprisingly two-dimensional. I might have run across Myles, but he's so shallow anyway that I wouldn't have noticed the difference."

She really wanted to punch him, but as her jailor, he might not respond well. "So you think you're in hell, but you're not sure. Do you really think holding me hostage will result in your freedom?"

"I just want my cane back."

*Bullshit.* "You may have stolen Baron Samedi's staff, but it never really belonged to you. The voodoo loas of the dead will rise up out of Guinee to fight you if you take it back."

He looked at her with the same smug countenance that he'd had in life. "I wouldn't rely on the loas if I were you. Those guys have peculiar ways of settling their differences. As you're my prisoner, there's no point in negotiating with you. I'm only here to make sure you're settled into your cell. Now all I need is for Sanguine to figure out that I've taken you." He nodded at her like a boy who'd shown his junk and expected her to open her pants and do the same. "I laid down my cards."

In spite of Sanguine's continued warnings about him needing to figure things out on his own, Kendell didn't see much point in denying the obvious. "The totem and golden guitar pick are the seventh gate between my real world and the hell dimension that Agnes created. Sanguine isn't among the living, so the gate is how I check in with her."

"Since I was able to use my trap to pull you through the gate, I must not be in your dimension. All that energy I released from the World Trade Center sent me flying between worlds, so I should have escaped hell, but I didn't, did I?"

*It's not like you didn't already know.* "As you said, the time for opening gambits is over. Myles used *his* cane to drive a totem containing a piece of my soul through different realities. Once we knew you were chasing us, we circled back around to hell. As for the people and things we added to Agnes's creation, that all gets too technical for me to explain. But everything you see is real, just without soul."

～

SANGUINE BOLTED out of the chair in hell's version of Scratch and Sniff and was airborne before she got out the door. If Myles had half a brain, he'd be racing for the speakeasy behind the Scratchy Dog at that very minute. The only logical answer to Kendell going unresponsive and as stiff as a board was that Colin had intercepted her soul. *I knew these stupid gates were going to be the death of us.*

She flew low among the buildings, less to avoid Colin than to prevent herself from moving in time. Being emotionally distracted while in flight could too easily cause her to look in the wrong time window. Her feet hit the pavement at the front door of the club. She ran through the building and out the back door then lifted the shutters that hid the secret bar. *Come on. Move it, Myles.*

An eternity later, sweaty and out of breath, he appeared behind the bar. "What just happened?"

"It must have been Colin. I've been keeping an eye on him, but he must have figured out how to tap into our communication. The only tools in this realm capable of that type of surveillance would be in the World Trade Center. Luther Noire has some explaining to do."

"How do we find her?" To his credit, he hadn't blamed her for the abduction but instead had gone right to the practical considerations.

"I have no idea," she said, "but I think it's time I came out of hiding. If Colin is too dense to realize he's not still in hell, Kendell will surely give it away."

"She's more clever than you give her credit for."

*Insulting a guy's girlfriend after she's just been abducted probably isn't the smartest way of enlisting his help.* "I didn't mean she couldn't keep a secret. She can handle herself when it comes to Colin, but if he's got her soul without the use of your cane, he'll know he's still got devilish powers."

"I'm coming to hell to help you find her." Myles's eyes were full of determination. He was clearly ready to risk everything just to save Kendell.

"Give me a day to figure out what he's up to," Sanguine said. "We can't risk having you trapped on this side with that magic cane. That would only put everything Colin wants right where he could get it. The last time you made the trip, you barely made it home, and we're still not sure who piloted the totem out of hell. If it *was* the ghost of Marie Laveau, you can't rely on her whisking you out of hell a second time. Come barging in here like a raging bull, and we could end up with Colin breaking down the walls again."

"Isn't that what he just did?"

Sanguine considered the question. She couldn't see what Colin was up to, but if he'd wanted to return to life, he probably wouldn't have dragged Kendell through the gate. "He's a chess player, and this was an aggressive move. If I confront him while wearing these wings, he'll know he's still in hell. But I don't see another option. Annie's body is useful for sex, but the time for emotional foreplay is over."

"What will that do for your vision of his possible future actions? I thought he needed to come to the realization he's still in hell on his own."

"That's another reason I need to *see* him," she said. "We're off script in terms of the possible futures I saw. I really thought I had his full attention by working that sex-bot."

"I don't think Colin is as easily led around by his cock as most men."

*I wasn't simply having sex with him, you fool. That's just typical male thinking. I was using sex as a way of opening the door to his emotions.* But she knew it wasn't the time to be arguing about her actions. "Apparently, he is a slave to his lusts, though." The comment wasn't meant to be mean-spirited, but she could see the pain she'd caused. "I didn't mean in the Baron Malveaux way of enslaving his adversaries' women. He craves the mental stimulation that is only possible by debating a woman. Kendell won't be harmed."

"I hope you're right. If you don't have her back to me by tomorrow night, I'm using my cane to cross into hell."

*That doesn't give me much time,* Sanguine thought. "There's one more thing. Until we know exactly how Colin hijacked the link I shared with Kendell, we have to be cautious using these gates for communication."

Myles looked around the speakeasy as if he expected to see Colin lurking in a shadowy corner. "You think he's had access all along?"

Kendell's arrogance in believing the gates could hold Colin, combined with her acceptance of Baron Samedi's assurances that their creation would be secure, had always mystified Sanguine. But Myles didn't need to hear about her skepticism of Kendell's trusting nature so soon after her abduction, so Sanguine chose her words carefully. "I just think we need to be more careful. If you and I realized this would be the next logical gate to use, so would Colin. It was less than a half-mile flight to get here. I suspect he's a little too tied up with Kendell's anger to break in on us now, but he'll figure out this is where we are. We need to be sneakier with our next choice."

She stared hard, willing him to keep quiet about any suggestion he might have. Even if Colin wasn't trying to abduct one of them, that didn't prevent him from listening in.

## 8

*C*olin stood in the parking lot that surrounded his condominium building. He'd been prepared for a fight. He just hadn't expected it to be with a winged goddess and her two guardian alligators.

Sanguine's outstretched wings quivered so quickly she looked like a hummingbird standing in midair. "Just answer me this: what was I to you?"

"I have no idea what you're talking about."

She hovered a good foot off the ground, which made her look taller than him. "Bullshit. You know full well it was me in Annie's body. Were you just toying with me to get Kendell's attention?"

"This isn't about making either of you jealous."

"Jealous? You think you've made me jealous? More like pissed off."

"I can see that. I'm not interested in Kendell. I only want my cane back." Colin was grateful that the people who walked past the parking lot were nothing more than marionettes. Had they been real, someone would be calling in a domestic dispute.

Her wings went still, and she settled to the ground. "You have to be fucking kidding me. This whole time you've been playing with me to get your magic wand back?"

"Can you say you've been any better in hiding behind some poor girl?" he asked. "I'm just now getting to see the real you."

Her alligators snuck forward on their bellies, probably in response to his harsh tone.

"I had my reasons, but nothing I ever said to you was a lie." She spread her wings to their full width. "One look at these, and you'd have known you were still in hell."

*Now you've also confirmed it, and since I'm holding Kendell captive, you can't know she's already told me.* "So what's your point in telling me now?"

She stared at him then looked off to the left as if he'd turned and walked away. "I had to wait until you figured out your situation without me giving it away. I know it may not seem like it, but I'm here to help you."

He laughed in derision. "By lying to me? Or do you see me as some puppy who just needs a chew toy to keep him pacified in his crate?"

"You're the one who is manipulating me to get your cane back. And if you can imprison your little crush while you're at it, all the better."

He considered storming off to his loft, but she deserved better. Plus, he still needed her help. "I never really gave a damn about what Kendell thought of me. I needed her to be open enough so I could make my case for getting out of hell. I won't lie by saying I didn't feel anything for her, but my time with you has shown me that it was only lust held over from the baron, combined with Lincoln's need to win. The conversations you and I have shared have been much more meaningful to me than you can know."

"Kendell's right. You're very good at turning on the charm when you need to. Why should I believe anything you say? Kidnapping Kendell proves you don't give a damn about me. You're always only out for yourself. No one else really matters to you. I should have done away with you like I'd planned."

So she hadn't already obliterated him from history. A glimmer of hope lightened his heart. "Why didn't you?"

"Changing time lines isn't possible. All I'd have done was create an alternate universe without you in it. Not that I'm opposed to such a world, but that wouldn't have prevented you from kidnapping my friend in the here and now."

Untangling what she truly felt for him was like trying to find a loose loop of a knot in the hopes of pulling out an end. "So you chose to rehabilitate me?"

She sneered at him. "I prefer your idea of giving you a bone so you'll stay in your cage. And by *bone*, I do not simply mean sex. We both know sooner or later you'll lose interest in me. Then, like an ill-behaved little dog, you'll start digging your way out again."

"What if I promised to never bother your reality if you help me retrieve the stick I desire? You, Kendell, and Myles can go on with your average lives and never have to worry about me or this hell for as long as you live." He watched her closely to see how she'd react. Returning to the living would mean leaving him behind. If she found an excuse to remain with him in hell, that would indicate an emotional bond deeper than she might be willing to admit.

She crossed her arms, but the combative posture in her shoulders and wings softened. "As the devil, you've proven not to be a man of your word. Or rather, you've found ways around your promises. How do I know you'd stick to the agreement?"

*Nice emotional counter move. You've neither jumped at being free of me nor made a lame explanation that you were required to stay on as my prison guard.* "My fight isn't with the living. The loas of the dead, however, have a lot to answer for."

"So you'd go back to being a harvester of souls in Guinee? No, thank you. I don't want you to end up in a position to replace those poor women you held prisoner in the afterlife."

"Then stay with me in this life." The words escaped his mouth before he knew it.

∼

SANGUINE HAD trouble preventing her wings from betraying her emotions. Whether she felt anger or desire, the appendages were like angelic lie detectors. They quivered as she tried to keep them folded behind her back. "Whatever future we might have can't even be discussed until you free Kendell."

"But you agree that a future together is possible."

She hoped the white feathers were able to hide the blush

that she felt in her wings. "Not so long as you continue to steal women's souls. You don't even have that cane, and you're already building your harem. How could I ever trust you?"

"Kendell isn't my slave. I've outgrown that segment of my existence. You must be able to see that. Have I ever tried to dominate you?"

*I'd like to see you try.* "You get more satisfaction in manipulating people than overpowering them, but I wouldn't put torture past you if you thought it would get you what you wanted. Let me see Kendell. I need to know she's unharmed. Until then, you can go whack off in your condo at your success at holding her prisoner." She flapped her wings as if preparing to leave.

"You know I wouldn't harm her, but I can't tell you where she is."

"Then we're at an impasse. I'm not helping you unless I get to talk with her, and we're not discussing any potential relationship so long as you keep playing the devil. I don't think we have anything left to discuss." She wanted to get as far away from him as possible.

"So you'd just leave your friend?"

She wasn't completely sure if he meant himself or Kendell. "I will always fight for my friends, but as a businessman, you'd be the first to tell me that when negotiations are at a stalemate, the two sides need time to reconsider their positions. So far, you've made a lot of arguments, but you haven't offered a path forward."

"Talk with Myles. Present my case. All I want is the cane, and in return, I promise not to reenter the reality you left.

As for us, I'll agree not to pressure you until I've earned your trust again."

His ability to so easily put his emotions for her aside only further enraged her and magnified her feeling of being used. She flapped so hard at the perceived insult that she ended up airborne. "I can't be around you right now."

Her wings flew her upriver without her giving the direction much thought. Flying gave her peace, even if she again had to resist the temptation to escape into an alternate time line. Nothing she did in the past would have prevented Kendell from being abducted in the present. Colin had conned Sanguine into letting down her guard, and that was something she could never forgive in a man.

But far worse than being played was the knowledge that he was right about her having to talk to Myles, and the sooner, the better. Myles might be a man of his word, but even so, she wouldn't blame him for fudging the twenty-four hours he'd promised her.

A flock of pelicans took turns diving into the river. She still had her animal militia at her service. *It can't hurt.* She directed the birds to patrol the river and look for anything unusual.

But putting her crew to work wasn't the same as freeing Kendell. *Where could he possibly be keeping her? The World Trade Center is off-limits. None of the embassies would allow him to stash a prisoner, and I've been keeping an eye on him. How did he do it?*

Anger renewed its hold on her emotions. *That's why you were toying with me. You wanted to distract me from your game.*

*Every morning when I left your loft, I turned my back on you. Stupid!*

She spread her wings and glided over the familiar swamps. As creator of hell, her grandmother wouldn't be of any help, but Sanguine desperately wished she still had the old woman to confide in. *I'm being a foolish, emotional little girl, just like he planned. That ends now.*

She turned away from the comfort of dreaming about her past and flapped her wings toward the Quarter. She and Myles needed to come up with a plan. Hopefully, Kendell was right, and Myles was more cunning than Sanguine had thought.

MYLES HADN'T LEFT his post at the fifth gate to hell from the moment Sanguine had flown off. *The last gate Colin would suspect us using would be the one we discussed, knowing he was watching.* Hopefully, Sanguine had the same thought. Every minute was an eternal agony. More than once, he'd wandered around the courtyard, resisting the urge to run home and grab his cane. Even if Colin did figure out that Myles could use the cane to enter or leave hell through the gate system, that asshole would not be able to exploit that knowledge if he were dead.

"Stop pacing. You're making me dizzy."

The sound of Sanguine's voice made him rush back to the bar. "What have you found out?"

"He has her, but I don't know where. He promises me she's safe. I believe him."

"What does he want?" Myles doubted there was anything he wouldn't give to have Kendell safely home.

"Your cane. He says he'll stay out of our lives—and by that I mean our world—if we give him the stick. I've already told him the loas wouldn't go for it."

*Damn that netherworld.* "If it were just about me, I'd let him have the thing. I never wanted it anyway, but giving it to him is one hell of a risk. Do you have any thoughts on finding Kendell?"

"No. And he won't let me talk to her. I suspect he knows I'd be able to locate her if I could establish a connection."

Kendell would tell him not to do something stupid, but he wasn't sure there was an option. "I can't sit here doing nothing."

"Agreed. I need your help in figuring out what to do next. That's why I'm back here instead of flying over the city, searching for her."

He knew they were in trouble when Sanguine admitted needing his help. "What are his weaknesses?" he asked.

Sanguine blushed. It was possibly the first time Myles had ever seen her do that. "I think he has feelings for me, though I don't know whether they're real or just another form of manipulation. Either way, he'll come running if I say so."

On the one hand, Myles felt horrible for endorsing Colin's pursuit of Sanguine as a way to distract him from Kendell. On the other, he was relieved that Colin wasn't trying to win Kendell over—he was just using her as a negotiating chip. "Do I dare ask how you feel about him?"

"At the moment, I could wring his neck. Up until he

pulled this boneheaded play, I thought we were making progress. His passing through the third gate and past his ex-wife seemed to confirm that he was evolving toward a person who could rejoin the human race."

From the way her wings sank below her shoulders, he could tell she held herself responsible for falling for his deception.

"Don't give up hope just yet. Changing a man whose dastardly deeds are legendary doesn't happen overnight."

She shook out her feathers. "Maybe not, but we still need a plan. We can't give him the cane, and that confines you to life. I guess I'm on my own out here."

He started pacing in front of the portal. "He hijacked her straight out of your conversation. That means the seventh gate is still open, at least from this side. Though, as we don't know where Kendell ended up, we have no way of knowing where that portal leads or even how to get someone else through it."

"Could you toss her a lifeline?" Sanguine asked. "You did a pretty amazing job preventing me from slipping out of existence."

Myles hated enlisting the band's help again. They had already suffered a lot of spiritual stress in trying to keep Sanguine connected to life. "I'll see what I can work up. What will you do?"

"Kendell's out here somewhere, but he's done a remarkable job of keeping her hidden. I'd have felt her presence if he'd have simply dumped her in hell, so she must be in some other dimension. We have to assume Delphine is still on our side, though it was her shop where the abduction took place. The only other person who plays around with alternate dimensions is Luther Noire. There's no point in you confronting him in life, but I'll cut that door down like the archangel Gabriel with his flaming sword if I have to. Whatever supernatural object Colin absconded with must have ended up on this side of the wall between life and hell."

Myles couldn't imagine Luther ever parting with anything he'd added to his collection. "It might not have been Luther's fault. If Colin did steal from the World Trade Center, he'd have needed some other way of accessing the vaults. Luther certainly wasn't going to let him in, and if Colin had broken in, Luther would have contacted us."

"Right. So the church is my first stop." She spread her wings. "Not like they'll refuse to let an angel into their sanctuary."

He made a mental note to check each of the faces of the carved angels in the cathedral just to be sure her holy visage hadn't somehow been captured in stone. "Just don't go giving them someone else to worship."

## 9

*M*yles waited at the gate until Sanguine had flown off to tackle her end of the plan. Even with her enhanced abilities, finding Kendell would be a long shot. Having a sexy angel in a diaphanous white goddess dress flying all over the city, however, would certainly attract Colin's attention. He lowered the green shutters over the speakeasy, fearing that his next contact with hell might not be so easy.

With the devil distracted, Myles hoped to create more than just a spiritual lifeline to Kendell. He walked into the club and pulled Charlie away from organizing the bar for the night's activities. "We're not opening tonight. I need you to find the band. Tell them it's about Kendell. We need to rescue her, and it's going to take everyone's help. And have Polly and Lynn bring Muffin Top and Cupcake. I'm headed home to grab Cheesecake and Doughnut Hole. Tell everyone to meet up at Delphine's as soon as possible."

Myles pedaled his bike as fast as the potholed streets would allow. Every minute, he envisioned Kendell in some cold, dark cell, scared and all alone. *Hang in there, my love. I'm sending help.*

He tossed the bicycle under the stairs of their apartment building and ran up the three flights. His leg muscles were burning from the exertion. When he finally opened the door, he saw Cheesecake lying on the ottoman, staring out the window and whining. Doughnut Hole paced in front of the French doors.

"Come on, dogs. We're going to go save Kendell."

Both pups ran over to him, barking with excitement. He grabbed his cane before hooking Cheesecake up to her leash and whisking Doughnut Hole under his arm. *Good thing Delphine's is closer than the club.*

When he reached Scratch and Sniff, he saw that Minerva's VW bus had already arrived. He entered the shop, where all four women and two dogs were nervously waiting for him.

"We've all been through this before," he said. "I propose forming the same spiritual bridge we did to strengthen Sanguine when she was saving Kendell. This time, though, we're going to connect directly to Kendell through the seventh gate."

Polly held Muffin Top close. "What about the pups?"

"Think of it like this. If Kendell had fallen through the ice into a lake, we would each hold hands and work our way out to grab her. That's what we're going to do now, but with her locked in an unknown dimension, we might not be able to pull her to shore. Even if that is the case, though, the pups should be able to use us as a bridge to her since they aren't originally from this dimension. If we can't pull her out of hell, the least we can do is send her help."

The women were lying next to Kendell's motionless body with all their heads together by the time he'd finished his explanation. Before he joined them, he addressed the four animals. "Once we build the link, I'm trusting that you pups will know what to do. Just follow Cheesecake's lead. She'll know right where to find Kendell."

As he performed his release from life, Myles experienced each of the women's souls as fellow links in a chain that extended from Kendell's motionless body at her seventh gate to an unknown solid barrier. He could feel the separation in dimensions like an abrupt change in temperature, but the wall was something new. The dogs took off across the human souls like squirrels running along a power line. At the solid obstacle, Cheesecake stopped in her tracks and started barking. The puppies, however, pounced through the wall as if it weren't there.

KENDELL HAD NEVER REALIZED how much she hated small, dark, scary places. She sat against a corner of the dimly lit cell with her arms around her legs, trying not to cry. Even focusing on her hatred of Colin failed to help her overcome her fears.

As she had when she was a girl, she closed her eyes and started singing "Bridge Over Troubled Water." The old Simon and Garfunkel tune so perfectly represented love to her that she imagined she was hearing Cheesecake howling along.

When the flurry of puppies jumped into her lap, she feared she was losing her mind, but their intense kisses hinted at another explanation.

"Myles must have found a way to get you through the portal." Crying was no longer something she resisted. "Where's your mama? That damn vault must be preventing Cheesecake from crossing over because she's not from this realm. You sweet, wonderful dogs. I missed you all so very much."

Doughnut Hole took up the duty that was usually Cheesecake's by cuddling tightly to Kendell's face and soaking up her tears with his shaggy coat. They were still the dogs Kendell remembered from life and not the hellhounds they'd been in Colin's realm.

"So that's how he's keeping me hidden. This box must have come from Luther, though he wouldn't have parted with it willingly. Hopefully, you dogs being here means Myles has figured out this box's origin as well. At the very least, when Colin opens that door again, he's going to be in for a shock."

She needed to find a way to prop the door open long enough for the pups to get out and revert to their hellish personas. They had already proven their ability to scare the crap out of any devil. She petted the scar on Muffin Top's nose. "You are all such brave puppies, just like your mama."

As much as she didn't want to let them go, Kendell needed to figure out what was in the vault that she could use to help the dogs escape. "I passed out when he opened the door. I guess mixing in another dimension must have overloaded my spirit. We need to figure out how to protect you guys from that same situation. If you have any ideas, I'm all ears."

As she started looking around at all the boxes, she began to wonder exactly how dumb Colin really was. From the psychic energy she felt radiate off each chest, she knew they were filled with Baron Malveaux's cursed items. She reached for a rough-hewn box, but her hand passed right through it. "Of course. I'm just spirit and not flesh." She turned to the door and pushed against it with all of her strength. "Damn you, Luther Noire. I can't grab anything inside the room, but I also can't get through these walls."

She slid back down to sit with the pups. "I don't imagine you guys came up with anything, did you?"

Doughnut Hole snuggled tightly to her side while the other two continued to explore their new cage.

She scratched the dog's ears. "At least I've got you guys. You just made my day a thousand percent better." She couldn't wait to give Myles a big kiss for understanding her needs even if he couldn't immediately rescue her. "I just hope Sanguine isn't doing something foolish like burning down hell in an attempt to save me. Or worse, killing Colin."

~

HELL HAD a way of providing for all of Sanguine's needs. She wondered if stacking the deck in her favor was a holdover from her grandmother, or if the old woman had managed to transfer hell's reins to Sanguine without her realizing it. Of course, when it came to the virtual overlay of cardboard people that Kendell and her gang had built in life for projection into hell, the rules were more understandable.

She held up the flaming sword. "So which are you? Did someone in life create you so I could possess you in hell, or did I think you up and make you real all on my own?"

Waves of crackling fire worked up from the hilt to the point.

"Or maybe you're just a manifestation of my anger at Colin. Whatever you are, those priests and monks hiding in their marble sanctuary are about to have their religion shaken to the ground."

Though she thought it a tad dramatic, she flew at the gates of the church with the blade pointed ahead of her like an avenging angel about to wreak her justice. As she approached the heavy wooden doors, they flew open, allowing her passage through the sanctuary to the altar at the front.

She put her bare feet on the purple carpet and held her sword up to light the room. "Someone had better materialize this instant, or I'm going to see if this sword can do more than just impress."

A monk in a black rope rushed out of the side office. "There's no need for all the theatrics. I assume you're here about Colin Malveaux. If you'll lower your sword, I'll show you what I showed him."

Sanguine felt a little foolish for having caused such a commotion, but performing the same act on Colin, as she would have liked, wouldn't have helped her free Kendell. The truth was, she was itching for a fight and never had liked the Church very much. Their having burned her ancestors at the stake had a way of souring her impression of the people in that institution.

"Of course," she said. "You just walked him right up to the World Trade Center fail-safe, didn't you? I'll bet you even helped him figure out how to use it."

The old man quivered in his robes. "Unlike you, he had the necessary credentials. When it comes to the supernatural, we respect the division of sacred from secular. As Luther Noire's objects aren't blessed by the Church, all I could do was make sure Colin was justified in making his claim."

Sanguine followed the monk down the dark, dusty passageway. "What did he take?"

"I'm not sure he took anything. He futzed with a control board, but I couldn't detect any change. He was only after what was his." The monk struggled to slide the marble slab partway off the sarcophagus. "I may not understand how this thing works, but we have our own divine intervention down here. If he'd tried to take anything that didn't belong to him, I'd have known."

She didn't want to know what type of magic the Church employed. The console inside the marble box didn't look as if it worked. "So all he did was flip a switch and leave?"

"He messed with all the switches and pushed a button, but in essence, yes."

"Any idea where the objects he requested ended up?"

The monk pushed the stone back in place. "Not my

department. You'd have to ask Luther."

*At least I now know how he did it. Maybe I can leverage that information to get Luther to be a little more forthcoming and not resort to his usual enigmatic responses.*

Sanguine left the church in frustration and flew at the World Trade Center again with sword drawn. The flaming blade melted the window to the floor of Luther's offices. She stormed down the hallway with her wings spread and blade drawn to look as intimidating as possible.

"Oh, it's you." Luther barely looked up from the stacks of papers that littered every available surface in the conference room.

"We need to talk. Colin has stolen his possessions—in case you hadn't noticed."

The man looked more haggard than she remembered. His clothes were wrinkled, his hair disheveled, and his sunken eyes looked as if they hadn't closed in a week. He lifted a pile of folders. "Do you have any idea what I'm up against? When that devil of yours had control of my building, he was setting off vaults like they were fireworks and it was the Fourth of July. Your witch cousins in Salem are having a field day with their returned brooms and caldrons. The city fathers up there are all up my ass to get things under control so they don't have to resume their witch trials." He picked up a royal-purple folder with a golden sash. "And look at this. It's from the queen of England, no less. The druids are forming an uprising. Don't those fools realize the capstone to Stonehenge was never meant to be used for barbequing chickens? You'd think for a group who prides themselves on knowledge, they'd know the difference between a ritual sacrifice and cooking lunch. Thank the ancients that Colin didn't figure out how to access the hidden vaults in the pyramids at Giza, or we'd be looking at another alien invasion. So you'll have to forgive me if I find the pilfering of a handful of men's jewelry boxes not my highest priority at the moment."

Though she could see his problem, she didn't honestly care. "Weren't the objects supposed to dump into the river in case of emergency?"

Luther tossed the file from the queen onto a stack of similarly colorful folders. "They would have if he'd used the main control panel. Since he locked out the vaults on the cabinets themselves, their resting places reverted to where the objects were originally discovered. Though their specific dumping location is dependent on a number of factors."

"Well I hate to *inconvenience* you, but if our shared nemesis isn't brought under control, he might decide to finish the job. He did figure out how to access the fail-safe."

That got his attention. "The monks are supposed to notify me in case of a breach."

She pointed at the mess of folders on the foldout table. "Maybe they have, and you just haven't gotten to it yet. Ever think of hiring a secretary?"

He searched through some loose papers. "I had one. She didn't prove trustworthy. Help me look for some handwritten document on Saint Louis Cathedral stationery."

"What's the point? He's already been down in the crypt."

He straightened up from leaning over the table. "What

do you think I'm doing here—updating my records? Each vault that's ejected from the tower creates its own microdimension. By being out of sync with everything in and around them, the vaults become impossible to detect. If I know where to look, though, I can pick up on their homing beacons. Think of a beacon as being like an airplane's black box pinging after a crash. The range isn't that far and grows weaker as the batteries fail. If Colin had used the central controls to eject the vault, there would have been a record letting me know where to begin my search. But he didn't, so in order to focus my efforts, I need as much information as possible on how he set the controls so I can find some clue as to where the iron box ended up."

Sanguine started digging through the closest pile of folders. "So if someone were held prisoner in one of those vaults, they'd be invisible to the rest of that dimension?"

"The vaults are designed to be the ultimate cage. Paranormal objects have a way of working themselves free from any confinement, so the vaults are like prison cells in space. Even if they're opened, anything inside will only escape into nothingness—at least while they're powered up. The battery life on those boxes varies depending on their size and how long they've been in this tower. Once the power dies, the vaults are no longer invisible. Then we have treasure hunters searching every country on earth."

Sanguine skimmed the documents in front of her. Most of them were more about the objects and the reason they were dangerous than where they might be located. A lot of the handwriting was hurried and the words filled with desperation.

"Kendell disappeared while I was talking to her over our hell's-gate link. Do you think Colin could have used his vault to snatch her?"

Luther tossed his latest folder on top of the one from the queen of England. "The vaults are purely isolation containers meant to maintain the objects inside. They can't reach out and grab any passing magical object. They aren't traps."

Sanguine thought Colin might have found a use for the vault that Luther hadn't considered. "But it is logical to assume he is using his vault as a jail cell to hold Kendell where she can't escape, so he must have had the vault deposited somewhere he could get to it."

Luther turned to a map of the river. Though it wasn't computerized, flashes of light appeared like lightning bugs along the coast. "See all these blimps? He dumped so many vaults in the river it's hard to know which one had his objects. The homing beacons are interacting with each other, giving me false readings. And as this realm of yours doesn't have real people, I'm finding it a challenge to hire an interdimensional excavation team to dredge the river."

"I can control the physical projections. Just let me know what you need, and I can put together a team."

"Again, the vaults don't work that way," he said with an air of exasperation that got on her nerves. "Your projects aren't of the same dimension. It takes someone from my reality to retrieve a vault. Since Colin was briefly in charge of the World Trade Center—and his vault contains his possessions—he can locate that one. It would show up in whatever reality he was in at the time he ejected it." He waved his pipe at the piles of folders. "There's a reason the vaults are being opened by practitioners of the paranormal. Now, if you're not going to help me, I have a ton of paperwork to work through and more agitated governments hitting me up by the minute. I'll contact you once I find Colin's vault. If you're right about him wanting the box itself, I'd start searching downriver. It's not like he could haul a closet-sized iron box around on his back."

"I just need to understand what to do if I do find the vault. How would I get Kendell out?"

"You wouldn't," he said. "You might not even be able to see the vault, though with your enhancements, I wouldn't hazard a guess on what you can and can't do. Most people wouldn't see the vault. They might even walk right through it. You'll be looking for something that isn't there, like a hole in reality. If you do somehow manage to locate it, you won't be able to open it even if the batteries have died. They're tuned to specific individuals' DNA." He again indicated all the files stacked on the tables. "That's one of the reasons this is such a mess. Since he ejected these vaults directly, they aren't locked the way they should be. Assuming he set the fail-safe correctly for his personal vault, only Colin and I will have access to its contents. If by some miracle you do find it, come back here and get me."

*And what if Colin realizes you're all that stands between him and every paranormal object you possess?* But Sanguine didn't need yet another impending disaster to distract her from finding Kendell. "I'll fly along the river with my helpers. If I find anything suspicious, you can bet I'll make a beeline back here. Be ready for me when I return."

## 10

*C*olin knew he'd set off a hornet's nest of activity by abducting Kendell's spirit. Negotiations often necessitated a certain amount of chaos. The process was like hitting a cue ball too hard on a pool table. The remaining balls' random trajectories could end up blocking his progress. However, the upside was that he might reveal an unexpected weakness in his opponent through the random collisions.

Pissing off Sanguine so completely, however, was like causing a billiard ball to ricochet so hard it kicked the cue ball off the table. Any game of manipulation required a degree of true emotion. His strength had always been his ability to care but, when the moment was right, to jettison the connection as easily as throwing out the trash. This time, however, the garbage can wouldn't empty. The danger had always been that he'd cram so much feeling into the limited space of his heart that love would jam itself tightly against the walls and refuse to leave. *I've played the game too long.*

Though time was against him, giving panic a chance to take hold of the team had its uses. He sat in his chair in the condo and watched the sun rise over the river. To be brutally honest with himself, he missed having Sanguine sitting next to him. In Annie's body, she was a fun play partner, but arguing with her in person cemented his feelings for her like concrete that had been poured around his galoshes and left to harden—and having her storm off was like being thrown in the river to drown.

He picked up the drawing of the baron's children and thought about the pipe tool in his pocket. From the moment Serephine had unintentionally killed herself with the pipe tool, he'd learned to isolate his love. But with Sanguine taking up so much space in his heart, even the hundred-year-old drawing brought tears to his eyes.

*Enough sentimentality.* Though he didn't yet have the magic walking stick, he needed to attempt entry into the bank Baron Malveaux had called home. Maybe he couldn't force Baron Samedi to come out into the open, but Colin's presence would certainly put the loa of the dead on notice. Surprise attacks had their uses, but so did the apprehension of knowing an adversary was taking aim. Baron Samedi was resting too easily in Guinee.

Colin rolled up the drawing to bring with him. The pastel had no business in his condo. It only served to remind him of a life that had never really existed.

Out on the street, the wind swirled around him as if nature itself were in turmoil. *How connected are you to this reality, sexy angel? And how can I use that to my advantage? Surely, you must find life boring after having commanded so much power in this afterlife. I know I do.*

He found it hard not to think about her. Without meaning to, he stopped at the confluence of white lines that delineated the parking spaces where he'd argued with her. He could nearly envision the differing events that had brought the two of them to that very spot just like the white painted arrows. *I'll see her again soon enough.*

As Baron Malveaux, he'd heard many dead souls lament their plight as the result of being distracted at the wrong time. Baron Samedi wasn't the type of spirit Colin would go against without his razor-sharp cunning honed to a clean edge. He walked through the parking lot without giving the markings another glance.

On entering the bank, he expected some form of recognition, but the workers toiled away like antique windup toys. Even the guard who stood watch to make sure none of the customers wandered into the inner offices looked more like a toy soldier than a real threat. Colin walked past him as if the man were made of stone.

"About time you showed up."

Colin felt the familiar cold shiver run down his back at hearing his mother's voice. He turned in to her office. "I didn't think you cared what I did."

"I don't, but as you are the heir to the Laroque fortune, I try to keep tabs on what's happening with you."

Colin had dealt with enough of Kendell and Sanguine's fake people to recognize a real human when he heard one. "And what do your spies tell you?"

"That you need my help."

He was grateful she didn't feel the need to rehash his recent history. The woman never did have time for discussing useless information. "If you know my situation, you'll understand why I ask how it is that you're here."

"You and the old baron weren't the only members of this family to consult with the voodoo priestesses. Delphine and I have an understanding: I don't interfere with her activities, and she keeps me informed regarding threats to my dynasty. When I received the voodoo-doll invitation, I knew it wasn't to a masquerade ball. She was sending me a warning. But it wasn't until Kendell and Myles showed up here, looking to enter Baron Malveaux's old office, that I knew something was up. That little guitarist and her dullard boyfriend aren't the brightest when it comes to subterfuge. I can't believe they're your primary adversaries." She held out her hands as if she'd never seen them before. "It didn't take me long to figure out how to operate this little toy. Your being cast into hell represents a sizable roadblock to our future—and a potential benefit. As you hadn't up until now tried to make contact with me, I assumed you had control of the game."

He'd never cared for her patronizing attitude. "What makes you think I'm here for your help?"

"You'd be a fool to try to take on the living and the damned without assistance. And you've never played the fool."

He sat opposite her behind the desk. "You know about Baron Samedi?"

She sighed in the exasperated way she'd done when he'd

been caught lying as a child. The problem was never the offense, but his having been discovered was unpardonable. "First of all, if you had really intended on keeping your union with our ancestor a secret, you should have continued with business as usual. Changing your name and walking away from your responsibilities removed any doubt as to your true identity. Since losing is never something you've accepted—either as Baron Malveaux or Lincoln Laroque—I knew the time would come when you'd challenge Samedi for control over Guinee. Personally, I find the whole escapade a waste of time and energy. Being a master of purgatory is like being a doorman at Walmart— eventually, you see everyone funneled through the gates."

"My goal was never just to rule the afterlife. Being able to resurrect the dead, however, would give me a control over people that's unequaled even by God himself."

She pushed her chair back from her desk. "Interesting."

"Why, Mother, that may be the first time I've seen you impressed by anything I said."

She put her fingers together at her mouth as if figuring out how to capitalize on his idea. "You're finally talking about something worthy of your heritage. A power like that would transcend wars, money, and politics. As the undisputed head of Guinee, would you be able to return people to life?"

"Not on its own. As you said, I did take over Guinee for a time. That victory was only the first step. Returning to life was where I failed. I came close, but possessing Myles's body wasn't sufficient. As you must have witnessed, inhabiting another person included too many pitfalls. Now that the baron and Lincoln are one in this body, I should succeed. But to move between dimensions, I need Baron Samedi's cane. Once I have that, I can return to Guinee to reassert my dominance. Then, when I walk among people again, it will be as a god. Now, tell me how all your money is going to help, because I'm not seeing how you're of any use at all."

He stood up and left the woman's office, grateful to have finally had the chance to tell her off. Her dominance over the son she'd never accepted as a man had ended. *Good luck being one of those I resurrect.*

The grand wood-paneled office was just as he remembered—no sign of Baron Samedi. With the help of Kendell and her team, Samedi had returned to Guinee.

"You might watch this seventh gate between life and death, but this hell is neither one. You were never welcome here, but I invite you back. Like boxers meeting before a fight, we should at least honor the niceties." He fell into the plush leather high-backed chair and let the drawing of his kids unfurl on the desk. The room felt like home. He kicked his feet up onto the desk and closed his eyes.

"Hello, Papa."

Though anything was possible in his private hell, Colin suspected he was dreaming his daughter's voice. If so, he didn't want to break the illusion.

Slowly he opened his eyes to ensure the spell remained. "Serephine?" His heart ached at the sight of his seven-year-old daughter standing next to her brother.

"It's me, Papa. Antoine said now that Mother gave you

the picture of us, we could come out of hiding, but only if you came to us. I missed you, Papa."

He didn't even want to blink for fear she might disappear. "I missed you too, my darling girl. What are you doing here?"

"We're here to save you." Her sweet, innocent voice brought back memories he'd suppressed long ago.

"Remember what we talked about, Sere." Antoine's tone made it clear that Baron Malveaux, in the form of Colin, wasn't going to get off that easily.

She turned her trusting big blue eyes toward her brother. "But we're here already. That must mean he's better now."

Antoine walked up to the desk and sat in the chair opposite Colin. Serephine joined her brother but remained standing slightly behind him as if needing his protection.

"Prove to us that you're worthy of forgiveness," Antoine said. "I want you to look into Serephine's eyes while you make your case. You never could lie to her."

Colin would have preferred trial by fire over having to look into his daughter's trusting blue eyes. "What happened to you was my first true sin. I should have been able to protect you."

Antoine drummed on the desk with his fingers. "You'll have to do better than that. She didn't die because you turned your back on her for a minute like an inattentive father. She killed herself over your deeds. That's the ugly truth you refuse to face."

"She died from the curse," Colin said. "There was

nothing intentional in how the blade slit her wrist. She was only a child."

Like a human lie detector, Serephine's face told a different story, though she remained silent.

Colin knew it was pointless to dodge the truth. "Maybe it doesn't matter. My sins were the basis of the curse, and Serephine was the first victim. I wish I could say that if it were possible, I would have lived my life differently so the curse would never touch you—either of you. But that person I was didn't see any roadblocks ahead, only opportunities for the taking." He looked into the sky-blue eyes of his daughter. "I've seen what was possible in an alternate reality—one where I didn't cause your death. But that man wasn't who I was as your father, and I've had to live with that knowledge for far too long. I would move heaven and hell to have you back."

Colin turned to Antoine. "As for you, I don't even have an alternate reality to go on. Every man must one day surpass his father. You did so at an early age. I bear no credit for the man you became, only guilt for causing the drive that made you protect our family from the curse for so long. There are no words capable of carrying the sorrow that I feel for my actions. You spoke of forgiveness. My asking for it would imply the possibility of you giving it, but you're not the only one who looked into the darkness of my soul. Even if you were such an advanced being that you were able to grant the ungrantable, I'd never be able to do the same. *I* am the judge who denies my pardon."

Serephine came around the desk and kissed him on the cheek. She then opened the top drawer of the desk and removed a pastel drawing hidden underneath. "This is so you won't forget. True forgiveness is a life-long journey, not a destination."

He looked at the page covered in renditions of the young girl's eyes. Each one seemed to stare straight into his soul.

~

COLIN JOLTED out of his sleep in the office chair. "I was dreaming."

His foot slid on the desk, causing him to momentarily lose his balance. When he set his feet on the floor and straightened himself up, he saw the old vellum sheet covered in drawings of Serephine's eyes. *This is still hell, and not everything is real. It would be just like Sanguine to mess with my emotions. Her manipulation of my feelings seems more plausible than meeting with my kids who have long ago passed into the* deep waters.

Even though he gave himself a plausible explanation, the drawing tugged at the love he'd long ago set aside. He pulled an empty file folder from the bottom drawer of his desk, put the two pastel drawings inside, and stashed it away in the top drawer.

"She was a lovely girl." Baron Samedi's familiar voice roused Colin from his emotional contemplation.

"So you're the one who conjured the ghosts from my past. It's still a little early for *A Christmas Carol.*"

Baron Samedi frowned and tilted his head as if considering the comparison of Colin to Ebenezer Scrooge. "It's not for me to say if you could be redeemed. As for the children, I didn't so much conjure them as allow them into your reality. You're familiar enough with time and dimension to not need an explanation. They were quite real."

Colin picked the drawing back up from his desk. "And what am I supposed to learn from this?"

"I'm only the ticket taker at the movie theater. But if you weren't here to see them, what are you doing back in the bank?"

*Why would you think I would know about them?* The yellowed vellum in his hands gave him the same feeling of peace as the pastel Fleurentine had given him. As she'd drawn both, he'd discounted his reaction to family sentimentality.

He reexamined the sheet. For some unknown reason, it reminded him of the plastic guitar pick. *Time for this later.* "Actually, I came to see you."

The voodoo loa sat back in the leather chair opposite Colin. "I can't imagine why."

"Call it professional courtesy. I'm going to retrieve *my* cane. Once I do, I'll be coming back to Guinee to reassert my authority."

Baron Samedi tilted his head and looked at Colin out of the corners of his eyes. "I've never known you to divulge your plan to an adversary."

"I'm hoping to avoid any unpleasantness. I've taken over your world once. You know I can do it again. I'd prefer a cooperative approach this time. Guinee isn't my final destination."

The spirit unfolded his legs and leaned forward, elbows on knees. "What are you up to?"

"We have a common oppressor—Papa Ghede. He's the one who set the rules of life and death a hundred thousand years ago. If I've learned nothing else in this hell, I now know death is not inevitable."

Colin could practically see the wheels turning in Samedi's mind. Overthrowing the supreme spirit wasn't something to take lightly. "That's why we're meeting here in your hell, isn't it? To wait until you've got the cane and then return to Guinee for the discussion would mean a one-way ticket to the *deep waters*—even for a loa of the dead. But again, why trust me?"

"I possessed that cane before, but I didn't have full use of its powers. You and Myles unintentionally showed me what it could do. We first met because you used that cane to leave Guinee for your Mardi Gras vacation. I should have seen then how you traveled between dimensions. Then Myles played the same game to make me chase Kendell around from realm to realm until I ended up back where I started in this hell. I'm not asking you to retrieve the walking stick for me. All I want is your assurance that you won't stand in my way. I know you're the one who limited its use."

The man's dark eyes didn't give anything away. "But if ruling Guinee isn't your objective, what are you up to?"

Forming a collaboration always carried the risk of the prospective partner taking all the power for himself, but as the one making the proposal, Colin knew he'd have to honestly divulge his plan if he was to gain Samedi's assistance.

"You and the other loas of the dead guard the seven gates, making entry into the *deep waters* a rite of passage all people must endure. I've spent enough time in your world to know not everyone seeks that privilege. With your walking stick, it's possible for a soul to move between dimensions. By using the cane combined with Delphine's voodoo totem, Myles has not only proven that concept, but he's also shown me that he can take others along for the ride. Of course, I can't bring people back from the *deep waters*, but I could rescue them from Guinee. The loas of the dead have no right to block the path back to life. Humanity has suffered death long enough."

"You must see that ultimately your plan would drain the *deep waters*. What happens then?"

*I'll rule over every human being.* But Colin didn't dare let his ultimate desire get the better of him. Some truths Samedi didn't need to know. "There will always be people who will choose death. Some lives aren't worth living. But instead of a boundless ocean, the reservoir of human spirits might become more like a lake. Would that really be so bad?"

"The *deep waters* are what connect all of the souls of the living. Without them, each of you would be truly alone."

*You fool, we're all already alone.* "We all have to make our own way through life. If the *deep waters* really connect us, then why are we so divided? Seems to me your idea of human existence doesn't work so well."

Baron Samedi conjured a clear glass filled with water covered by a thin layer of oil. "For most of human existence, this has been the balance between the living and the dead. Individuals were such a small percentage of the whole human spirit that each was able to connect directly to the water below." He waved his hand over the glass. Though the overall amount remained the same, the percentage of oil increased to a point where only the bottom of the layer of it was in contact with the diminished amount of water. "The population on earth has been growing exponentially. Your science states that seven percent of all humans who ever walked the earth are alive today. Now figure in how much of that *deep water* is continually reused—what you would call reincarnation. Too many living with not enough dead means some individuals have trouble accessing the love they need."

*Don't preach to me about love!* "Have you considered that if we were all out here together in life instead of depending on our ancestors to smooth the way, maybe we'd figure out our existence on our own? We would get along just fine without your meddling from the afterlife. Who are you to decide when someone's time is over? Given the option, there are a number of people I'd have liked to see hang around longer." He involuntarily touched his cheek. The memory of Serephine's kiss threatened to make him lose control of his emotions.

"And you would set yourself up as *God*—deciding whose life should continue and whose should not? Papa Ghede's answer was to treat everyone the same—all people die regardless of their deeds—but even he knew the decision to return a spirit to the *deep waters* was more than one being could handle. Guinee may not be the ideal purgatory, but it serves the purpose of deepening the interface between the living and the dead. Your plan would drain our realm."

*Now we have it. You'd lose all your power over humanity.* "Who set you up as judge and jury of people's souls? You condemn people. I would save them."

"But for what purpose? Your personal history doesn't inspire confidence that you'd make a benevolent ruler."

Colin hoped the satisfaction he felt wasn't betrayed by the smile he felt tugging at his cheeks. "If we're down to considering my credentials, you must at least admit my plan has merit. Humanity has a right to decide its own destiny."

"You don't represent humanity. If people reproduce faster than the *deep waters* can be replenished, that is out of our hands. The loas of the dead don't have a say in how fast people die. Just within your lifetime, the number of people wandering the earth has more than doubled. You say people will figure out how to get along, but even given the current gradual pace of the unbalancing of the living and the dead, your proposition would appear to be failing. If you put a sudden stop to death, how long before civilization degenerated into chaos?"

Colin balled his fist under the desk. "We don't need some outside rulers dictating our reality like we're their pet dogs."

Baron Samedi removed his top hat, pulled his handkerchief from his pocket, and wiped the white-painted skull from his black face. "I'm not an alien creature. Like all the loas—and Papa Ghede himself—we were people just like you. We dictate nothing. Our mission is to maintain the structure of human existence. What each person experiences, in terms of our mutual connection, is added to the *deep waters* on their death. What they discover and create in life becomes a part of the human experience. For humanity to evolve, there must be death. Choosing who lives and who dies deprives the future of growth. Besides, human bodies grow old, get injured, and fail. Simply putting a soul back into a dead body won't resurrect the person. It will only prolong the agony of their passing."

Colin sat back in his chair. "I never said I wanted to return them to that failed attempt at a dimension. Between the old dead swamp witch, her granddaughter, and Kendell's gang, I'm living in the perfect solution. The projected human puppets they've used to fill my world will no longer be soulless zombies. And with my control of this realm, people will no longer need to worry about the human frailties you've just described. All I need is the ability to rescue their souls from your purgatory."

## 11

Kendell had never fully appreciated how boring life could be with nothing to do and no one be with. The puppies were her salvation. Though not the best conversationalists, they were beings for her to talk to. "I never realized how bad this hell must have been for Colin. He spent years with little more than I have in this box."

Doughnut Hole laid his head on her knee.

"True, he could touch things. But you know what I'm saying. There was nothing for him to *do*. I might have chosen death if I'd been stuck in that reality with little hope of escape."

She focused her energy and tried again to pick up the box on the lowest shelf. Again, her hand passed right through. "This is so frustrating. If I could just move the box closer to the door and use it to block it open once Colin returns, you pups could get out and attack him."

Doughnut Hole barked at her once then turned to his sisters. At first, Kendell thought the dogs just needed a little play time, but when they formed a doggy chain up her body to the shelf, she wondered if they had something else in mind.

To her shock, the little black dog nudged the box off the shelf and onto the floor with his wet nose.

"Of course. You were born in this hell, so you're not just spirits. That's why you could cross over but Cheesecake couldn't." She ruffled the curly hair on his head. "You're such a good dog. Now, see if you can move the box over to the door." She hoped the pups' ability to interact with the objects in the vault would also mean they wouldn't pass out when the door between dimensions was opened.

But instead of pushing the box along the ground, the dogs circled it and started sniffing at the top as if there were doggy treats inside.

Cupcake lay on her belly and pawed at the catch.

"It's locked," Kendell said. "Luther wouldn't just close the box with a simple latch. I know you're magical creatures and all, but you're not going to pick that lock with your claw."

Cupcake growled softly but didn't turn away from her study of the small treasure chest.

A familiar bark from inside the box made Kendell jump from the floor.

"Cheesecake? What the hell's going on?" Each beat of her heart came on so strongly she feared her spirit would burst. *My girl can't be trapped in that box!*

"Don't freak out, Kendell." At least Myles's voice proved her beloved dog wasn't alone.

"I don't understand. What's happened to my dog? Where are you?"

"Cheesecake is just fine. We're using those cufflinks you talked about as walkie-talkies. Once Luther had control of the World Trade Center, one of his first tasks was dismantling the time machine Colin had built. Since Colin used his cufflink as his connection to the one he gave you, Luther put it in the vault with the rest of his stuff. And even though we couldn't reach you—and the cufflink we put in the voodoo totem is still in that hell dimension— Cheesecake and I are able to access it while in this psychic trance. The totem is still physically in Delphine's shop. Fortunately, the store is an interdimensional embassy. Apparently, though, we had to wait until the puppies turned on the power to the cufflink on your end before we could connect."

Kendell wasn't sure she cared how they did it. "I'm just so glad to hear your voice, both of you. I'm in some metal box. I assume it's one of Luther's vaults. Beyond that, I have no idea what's going on. My hand just goes through all of the objects in here, but the puppies can interact with them. Colin's after your cane."

"I know. That's why I'm not there, kicking his teeth in for abducting you. I can't get there without the cane, and bringing it there seems like something you'd object to. Sanguine did a pretty good imitation of you in describing why I shouldn't do something stupid."

Kendell laughed for the first time since being

soulnapped. "Like building a bridge to me with your spirit wasn't dangerous?"

"Oh, it wasn't just me. The band is lending me their essences as well. The bigger problem is that your soul is on that side of your gate and your body is here in life, which means the door is wide open. I wasn't just trying to send you puppy support. Me and the band are jamming the passage with our souls so Colin can't just walk out of hell."

Kendell could imagine Myles and the band lying comatose on the floor of Delphine's shop. "And laying your souls down in front of our enemy was the best plan you could come up with?"

"*My* plan was to bust into hell and beat Colin over the head with my cane until he told me where you were, but Sanguine convinced me that wouldn't be the brightest move. As for blocking an open gate between dimensions—if you've got a better idea, I'm listening."

Kendell pulled the pups close as substitutes for Myles. "I suppose you're right. I keep wondering why he didn't just move through the gate as soon as he abducted me. He must have known it was open."

"We've been a little busy on this side to question his motives beyond wanting the cane. I just assumed he wanted to fight on his home turf. Here in life, he'd be facing me, the band, the dogs—the list of adversaries is long. There in hell, I wouldn't have much backup other than Sanguine."

Kendell had to consider the possibility that Colin was just playing with them—again. "The voodoo loas of the dead have always been very clear that a soul must pass through all seven gates in order. And for a time, Colin as Baron

Malveaux was the guardian of the seventh gate. You don't suppose he knows something we don't?"

"Like maybe if he just walks through the seventh gate without first going through the six in order, his body and soul would be shredded to bits as if he'd been tossed into a wood chipper? Because if that's the case, I'll pull the band out of this connection right now and start waving the cane in his face through your gate."

Though Kendell shared Myles's desire to be rid of the devil, Colin, in full possession of his faculties, was far too clever to fall for such an obvious ploy. "Whatever he's up to, it doesn't appear to involve returning to the land of the living—at least not as his next move."

"Now you're going to tell me to let go of your soul so I can get back to work thwarting whatever devious plan he's got going."

She smiled at knowing him so well. "Then you'll tell me there's no way you're leaving me in this jail. We both know how this discussion ends. We can't just rely on Sanguine finding me, and you hiding from Colin won't get me any closer to being freed. Since he hasn't tried getting through the gate, there's not much point in you stuffing it with your souls. I just wish I could give you some idea of where I'm being held captive. I can't hear anything outside of this box."

"Makes sense. That vault isn't a part of either the hell dimension or this life. I'd go check with Luther, but Sanguine was headed that way when I built this psychic bridge."

Kendell hated the prospect of losing her connection to

Myles. "Do you think it'd be okay if the puppies stayed with me?"

"I don't imagine they'll be willing to leave. I love you, Kendell, and I won't rest until you're free."

~

MYLES FELT as if his muscles hadn't been used in a week. He found it hard to sit up from the hardwood floor. "I wonder if this is what it feels like to grow old. Because if it does, I'm going to stop ribbing my parents at Thanksgiving."

The band wasn't moving any faster. "Where's my dog?" Polly asked.

"The puppies stayed with Kendell," Myles said. "Cheesecake couldn't make the transition as she isn't from hell."

The elder dog sniffed at Kendell's body and whined.

Lynn only managed to sit up on her elbows. "What about Kendell? Did she learn anything useful about her cage?"

Myles wished he had more to tell them after once again using their spirits. "She's scared but okay. Colin hasn't returned to her, so whatever he's up to doesn't involve trying to seduce her. The vault must be in hell for him to have opened it, but as it's from Luther's building, it's not really anywhere."

"So we could find it as easily as Sanguine could?" Polly asked.

Myles suspected the search would be pointless. *At least it'll give everyone something to do.* "Anything beats just sitting around, waiting for Colin to make his next move. Sanguine was going to check in with Saint Louis Cathedral about the fail-safe before heading to the World Trade Center, so there's not much point in retracing her steps."

Polly looked around the small room. "Using Kendell's gate would be like being on hold with a utility company. So it's not likely that Sanguine would try to contact us here, but how do we pick which gate to watch?"

Myles finally got to his feet. "Sanguine has never been the most punctual or predictable. This time, if we want to talk to her, we would need to contact her, and that means a long drive out to the swamp."

Minerva pulled her keys from her canvas bag. "Good thing I brought my VW, but that will only get us to the bayou outlet. We'll need some way to get through the swamp, and from what I recall, that's not so easy."

Myles didn't really want to make the trip just to hear what he probably already knew. "If anyone has an alternative idea, I'd be really amenable to anything that moves us along faster."

Scraper leaned against wall. "Has anyone considered *how* he moved that vault? The thing is the size of a small closet. Even with his devilish powers, he'd need help."

Myles had been so focused on the vault's resting place he hadn't considered how it had arrived. "From what I gathered about the fail-safe, the vaults were supposed to end up in the river to avoid a meltdown. He must have moved it so Luther wouldn't immediately know where it was. The way the tides run around here, though, we couldn't be sure if he moved it upriver or downriver."

"Either way," Minerva said, "he'd need someone with a

boat. As the people in his realm are simply projections, shouldn't we be able to play back their actions like rewinding a film?"

Myles's body hurt so badly that he didn't really want to hike down to the river. "Sounds like we'll need that ride after all, except down to Professor Yates's laboratory."

∾

As MYLES ENTERED the office on the river, he had never been more hopeful of the crazy professor having something useful up his sleeve. The room's combination of mad-scientist lab and steampunk gallery would have made Jules Verne envious. "You must be getting ready for a Halloween show."

The professor never was the most organized with office décor or personal appearance. He ran his hands through his wiry gray hair. "Most of this stuff is to keep up our apparitions in hell. The drinks your friends are pouring for patrons all around the city are generating so much psychometric energy that I'm having trouble keeping up."

Together with the professor and the four band members in the cramped office, Myles was having trouble finding a place to lean without triggering some piece of equipment. "I know it wasn't part of the plan, but we're hoping there's some way to see what happened along the river a week ago. Colin got his hands on one of Luther's vaults, and we need to find it. Kendell's soul is locked inside."

Professor Yates didn't ask for an explanation but instead started playing with a bank of equipment that occupied the wall along the hallway. "Here's the problem: I can isolate a section of that realm and run it backward, but I don't know what Colin will be seeing in his hell. He might see exactly what we see on our hologram. Of course, events won't be going back in time. If he moved the vault, it'll stay right where it is, and as he's not one of our puppets, you won't see him. All we'll see are the virtual-reality people and objects that we're projecting. But if someone helped him, like you believe, we should see something that doesn't make sense."

"Do it," Myles said. "By now, he must know he's in hell. He's already seen Sanguine with wings, so what do we have to lose?"

A three-dimensional projection of the French Quarter lit up between the paperwork and small machinery on Professor Yates's worktable.

"Just put that equipment and those files on the floor. I'll run the projection from here. If you see something suspicious, I can move things forward and backward like a movie reel. First I'll reset the figurines to a week ago."

Myles arranged the women around the table. "We want to figure this out fast—before Colin gets the idea we know where he has stashed Kendell. I wish I knew what to look for, but if anything seems strange, don't hesitate to say so."

The women leaned in over the projection. "Just start up this diorama," Polly said, "but go slow to begin with so we can get a feel for how it works."

For an hour, Myles stared at the holographic rendering as if troubleshooting an intricate Victorian mechanical toy to bring it back into working order.

"What's that?" Lynn asked.

Myles got down on his knees to inspect the section of river she was looking at. "I don't see anything."

She pointed to a patch of river lit by the moon. "That rectangular section of water looks translucent, and it's moving in time with that pilot boat."

Myles let the professor run the image until the water patch moved under the wharf at the end of the working docks and the gang lost sight of it. "Good eye, Lynn. I'd never have caught that. Professor, run the movie backward for a bit."

Now that he knew where to look, Myles caught sight of the section of mysterious water emerging from under the concrete landing and working its way back to under the World Trade Center. When the boat swung around and the rectangular light-gray water anomaly disappeared under another overhang, Myles had the professor stop the projection and run it forward again. "Looks like we found out where it was dumped after he used the fail-safe, and its final resting spot as well."

Polly shook her head. "I'd like to see the next few days. Colin had to be inside the box when he abducted Kendell, and that would be awfully difficult if that vault was still underwater."

The whole gang huddled around the projection as Professor Yates increased the speed. As a day passed on the diorama, Myles worried that they were taking a needless risk. All Colin would need to do was look out at the river, and he would see people and boats moving in fast motion.

But when Myles again saw the rectangular hole in the water, he knew Polly had been right. "There it goes. I don't see any boat that it might be attached to this time. You don't suppose Colin was riding on top? There's no way I would go shooting down the Mississippi on something I couldn't see or control." The water anomaly disappeared into a thicket along the levee.

Minerva pointed through the trees that lined the river. "There's a shipwreck below those limbs. When I was in high school, we'd use it as a make-out spot. You can walk to it at low tide. Based on the size of that water anomaly, the wreck would be plenty big enough to house that vault."

They all watched intently, but they couldn't make out any more of Colin's activities through the dense vegetation.

Myles's body still ached from lying on Delphine's floor. He put his hands on his hips and stretched out his back. "Looks like we have a location. If no one has any objections, I think we can return Colin's hell to its normal programming."

Everything along the river of the diorama switched back to the way it had been. Professor Yates came out of the hallway. "Simply knowing where the vault is won't get you inside it. It's not just invisible in hell—you won't see it in life either."

*What if I kidnap Luther and force him to open it?* Myles knew the thought was irrational. The stress of having Kendell imprisoned in hell was getting to him. Luther was Sanguine's responsibility, and even if he weren't, it wasn't as though Myles could break into the World Trade Center and force the man to do anything.

yles left Professor Yates's lab to do some thinking while staring out at the river. He felt completely lost without Kendell around to help him make sense of what he knew. His history of crossing dimensions was one big jumble of experiences, which made it even harder to come up with a plan for rescuing her.

Polly caught up with him on the concrete bench. "Where to next, fearless leader?"

"I wish I knew. Heading down to the shipwreck won't do us much good if we can't see or feel the vault. We wouldn't even know if it was there, let alone get it open. And even if we did open it, I'm not sure how Kendell would cross between dimensions. Honestly, this whole interdimensional-connections crap gives me a headache. I don't even know where to start." He hated sounding so pessimistic, but he had to speak honestly. If anyone would understand his emotional state, it would be Polly.

She stared out at the water. "You and Kendell are the experts at all this paranormal stuff. Me and the band are happy to help, but I'm afraid when it comes to what you two have been doing, it's like watching two mathematicians solving some advanced calculation. I can't even make sense of the symbols. Who do you trust who might be able to help us figure these things out?"

Working through a problem helped him keep his emotions in check. "It might be easier to list who I *don't* trust, and why. Delphine is the most knowledgeable regarding all things voodoo, but she had a lot to do with getting us into this mess by tempting Kendell into pursuing voodoo. Honestly, I'm still dubious about how much Delphine knows when it comes to anything other than voodoo."

Polly rubbed her bare arms against the October chill. "She did help form the virtual overlay to hell, but other than that, she's been pretty useless. We need someone who really understands the nature of other dimensions, not just the one."

Myles was somewhat relieved Polly didn't argue him into keeping Delphine on the list of potential counselors. "The Church has probably more history with other dimensions than any other organization, including Luther's, but they're not exactly forthcoming with information."

"They give me the creeps. I hate being preached to, and I always feel as though if I say the wrong thing, they're going to condemn me—or someone I love—to hell. Who's next on your list?"

"Luther Noire—"

Polly cut him off. "Come back to him later. I suspect he's where we're going to end up, but I'd really rather find a less biased source of information."

"Agreed, but the list is starting to get a little thin. Sanguine is good at working the system, but she's not her grandmother. Agnes Delarosa not only understood other dimensions, but she built hell as well. Unfortunately, I'm not that good at talking to the dead."

Polly looked across the river and tilted her head as if she'd just noticed something. "What about Mary? She greeted us when we took that VW ride into hell, and she let us use her plantation as the first gate. I never gave it much thought at the time—mostly because I didn't have a clue as to what was going on—but how did she know to find us?"

The sweet old woman had seemed so nonthreatening that Myles had simply accepted what she'd said without question. He tried remembering the various other interdimensional doorways he'd used. "She is unique in our meetings with people from other dimensions. We did meet Serephine in Anthony Laurette's old mansion, but we had to find the interdimensional trap door first."

Polly turned to him. "And we met with Miss Fleur in the convent, but as it's part of the Church, that's not surprising. Between these gates and embassies, I get confused about the rules."

Myles nodded, less in agreement than from the knowledge sloshing around in his brain. "I know what you mean. The Mary we know in this dimension was very friendly toward Kendell, and she did claim to be a seer. I know she'd meet with us, but I don't know if she's as knowledgeable as her interdimensional counterpart."

Polly got off the cold bench and offered Myles her hand. "It's a place to start. Worst case, we end up back at the World Trade Center. I'll happily take a pleasant conversation and a cup of homemade gumbo from Mary over Luther's sneer of self-importance and day-old beignets any day, even if she is crazy."

~

MYLES KEPT his eyes closed as Minerva coaxed her old VW up onto the Crescent City Connection. His memory of the poor underpowered bus being souped up to handle the drive over the same bridge made him grip the overhead rubber handle. On that trip, they had arrived in hell. He was slightly relieved when she downshifted into second gear for more power instead of up into the paranormal fifth gear for dimensional crossing.

Polly nudged him in the side. "You can relax. She doesn't have that silver-skull gearshift handle—not that it would work."

He relaxed his grip on the handle, feeling just a little bit foolish for the unsubstantiated fear. "I don't think I'll ever get used to puttering around in this breadbox."

When Minerva took the exit, Scraper pointed toward a Rouses grocery store. "We should pick up some food for Mary's clan. Seems like it would be rude for all of us to show up expecting a meal without at least helping out where we can."

Myles pulled out the credit card Kendell had gotten for the Scratchy Dog. "Fill up a cart. Anything more than that, and they might be offended. As they're still living among the trees, they won't have a fridge, so stick to nonperishable items."

He'd never really appreciated how fast four women could fill a cart or how they could pick the most expensive items, but if the shopping spree resulted in useful information, the splurge would be worth it. With the bags loaded into the back of the van, they headed out to the homeless enclave along the river. The bus's suspension groaned when Minerva drove over the levee and onto the grassy tree-lined batture.

Mary ran out of the cottonwood grove to meet them. "I'd know the sound of the old VW engine anywhere. We're just finishing lunch, but I'm sure there's enough jambalaya left in the pot to fill your stomachs. For some reason, I managed to make more than we needed today."

Myles and the band carried the plastic bags loaded with provisions through the dense vegetation to the camp made up of tarps and discarded lumber.

Mary made sure each of them was comfortably seated around the constantly burning bonfire. The piping-hot bowl of food she handed Myles smelled of shrimp and rich Cajun spices. Though there was work to do and they had questions that needed answers, he took his time, savoring the first few spoonfuls of rice and seafood.

Mary sat between Myles and Polly. "What's happened to Kendell, and how can I help?"

Myles felt encouraged by her intuition that Kendell was in trouble. "She's been abducted into a hell dimension. We're hoping you can help us figure out some of the details. You called yourself a seer. What did you mean?"

Mary set her bowl on the ground and wiped her mouth with her apron. "Most people understand that if they're faced with a choice and pick one direction, in some alternate reality, they might have gone the other way. Typically, that awareness is just philosophical, and no one really pays much attention. A seer, however, can connect to the versions of her that took the other directions. Each branching creates a twin, and like siblings that have shared a womb, we have our special awareness of each other."

The food was so good that Myles almost regretted scarfing it down so fast, but with Kendell in trouble, he felt guilty for taking any more time than necessary on culinary pleasures. He set the empty bowl aside. "We understand that with each direction picked, an alternate dimension is created. What we really need to understand is how those realms interact."

Mary sat quietly for a minute as if she'd slipped into a trance. "Are you referring to the interdimensional embassies?"

"The embassies," Myles said, "but also the gates. I've traveled between realms, but it was always based on someone else telling me what to do. No one bothered explaining the process. To find Kendell and rescue her, we're going to need to know what's going on. There aren't many people who understand how to cross dimensions, and fewer that I trust. It seems to me that the version of you we met in hell occupied both an embassy and a gate."

Mary snickered. "I told you I'd know that VW sound anywhere. It takes a skilled seer, but some of us can not only detect what's happening parallel in time, but also follow along with events in the past. A really gifted person can even read the near future, but those people have to keep their skills a secret. Too many prophets end up with tragic lives that are cut short by unimaginative institutions. As you might guess, embassies are often set up by seers because we're at ease looking into other realities."

Polly added her empty bowl to the growing stack on the ground. "So we know people from the different dimensions can meet in an embassy, but can they exchange items or even cross over themselves? We know Colin was able to take some of Delphine's totems from her shop into his hell because it was an interdimensional portal."

"Each seer establishes her own rules with her alternate self, though transferring anything from one to the other is unusual. I've never heard of a person walking into an embassy from one dimension and out the embassy from another. To do so physically would scramble a person's memories. If she weren't a seer, she'd likely go insane."

*Great,* Myles thought, *so I can't just walk from this cottonwood grove into hell. Though even if I could, I still wouldn't be able to see that damn vault.* "Is there a connection between the embassies and the gates?"

"Gates are far more complicated. As you used me for the first gate between your reality and hell, I won't bore you with specifics you already know. The gates started when certain people who were familiar with the embassies got a little put out that they couldn't be in charge. They set up the gate system as a competing connection between realities. A person who approaches them correctly may travel between realms through the gate system, even though they can't through the embassies."

"You mean the loas of the dead built the gates as a challenge to your embassies?" Myles asked.

"Those voodoo loas never liked that a person couldn't travel through an embassy. Their system is a little too controlling for my tastes."

Polly held her plastic cup of sweet tea. "What about the gate guardians? Can they go back and forth between dimensions?"

"Only the one in charge of the seventh gate. All of the other gates are preliminary tests. But if that guardian—either Kendell or Baron Samedi—goes through the passage without some way of holding the door open, they'll become stuck on the other side." The matronly homeless woman stared into the fire. "Like the embassies, the gates are mostly useful for talking to the other side. Humans really aren't meant to leave their designated realities."

Lynn got up and warmed her hands next to the fire. "Aren't you both an ambassador and a gatekeeper?"

"I agreed to Kendell's request to be the first-gate guardian partly to help her and partly out of curiosity. I'm afraid I may have failed her in letting Colin pass, but being a seer doesn't always come with twenty-twenty future vision."

Myles could imagine Sanguine saying much the same thing. *She must be the seer in charge of hell. Why didn't I realize that?* "So a person can't travel between dimensions through an embassy and can only do it through the gates if all seven are used correctly. Then how did we drive to hell?"

"Voodoo and Wicca each have their own rules. Imagine two friendly counties who have a bunch of embassies on each other's lands. There would always be situations where people would have to travel from one county to the other. Agnes Delarosa built the hell dimension, but Marie Laveau was heavily involved in the design. As Marie's descendent, Delphine was able to create a voodoo passage to hell by using the two pieces of Baron Samedi's cane. She was lucky to have such a powerful object from Guinee as her talisman in both life and hell. Such trips can be quite risky. People traveling between dimensions have a way of creating all kinds of horror-story myths. Frankenstein's monster, for example, was just some poor dude who lost his memory and got torn up physically by using electricity to cross dimensions. Mary Shelly wasn't the best seer I've ever known. That's also how we ended up with stories about time travelers."

*Great, another strikeout.* "What about Baron Samedi? He was able to travel from Guinee to life, but then something went wrong when he went to hell."

Mary tossed a log on the fire. "Samedi and those loas are idiots. He never should have gone to that first Mardi Gras. Any seer knows not to go wandering around in another

G.A. CHASE

dimension like a drunk tourist on Bourbon Street. He deserved to lose his cane to Baron Malveaux. But to get to your question about his trip to hell, Agnes Delarosa's hurricane was so powerful Samedi got sucked into it. He was like a brick that got hurled so hard it punched a hole in the wall between the two realms. When he returned to Guinee, the hole was patched. This is the kind of thing that happens when there isn't a seer in charge."

Myles feared how Mary would take the news about his journeys between realms. "Papa Ghede gave me Baron Samedi's cane. I've used it to enter Guinee and even reopened the door from Guinee to hell so Kendell could enter and save Sanguine."

Mary poured some bourbon into her sweet tea and offered it to the others. "That probably wasn't the smartest move on your part, but I understand why you did it. Love is a whole different brand of magic, and it's beyond my understanding. I've seen stupid ideas succeed because of love and brilliant schemes go down in flames because of a lack of human connection. I can only tell you how things are supposed to work. Even the loas know better than to allow someone to bodily pass from one dimension to another. That hole Samedi created when he passed into hell must be worse than I thought if you were able to open a gateway such that Kendell was able to walk through it."

The added alcohol quieted some of the fears that were rearing up in Myles's imagination. *Score one for love, but no one's offered me a magic love potion for saving Kendell.* "But it is possible to travel between dimensions without using an embassy or the gates."

Mary sighed and pulled a crocheted shawl around her shoulders. "People have been making magical objects—both intentionally and by accident—from the time Cain killed Abel with a stone. As the first human death, Abel might well have been the first person to transfer to another dimension. You're the psychometry genius. Can you imagine what kind of energy must have been left in that rock?" She nodded at the World Trade Center across the river. "Luther Noire has made collecting those little trinkets his specialty. The problem with using a magical object to cross dimensions is there's no way of knowing where, when, or in what form you'll end up. Again, we're talking horror-story monsters and science-fiction villains. Fortunately, there aren't many magic practitioners clever enough to create objects powerful enough to cross dimensions. As a seer, each time someone breaks into my realm, I create stronger protections against it happening again. That's another reason we formed the embassies—mutual dimension protection."

Myles knew all too well what she meant. "And Luther has been gathering all those objects like a kid stockpiling firecrackers before New Year's Eve. Colin has already tried setting off the vaults to blow a hole between his hell and our life. It's those dimensionally sealed cabinets that are our problem. Kendell's being held captive in one. Colin ejected the box containing his cursed items into hell. Now we have no way of finding it or figuring out how to open it. He's demanding Baron Samedi's cane as ransom for Kendell's soul."

"Luther and his stupid vaults are going to be the end of

us all. He thinks he's so clever. The secret to his containment fields—and that includes the vaults themselves —is that they aren't actually in another dimension, though he likes to imply that they are. Everything he uses, from the cement that went into the building to the iron that makes up the vaults, is slightly out of phase with whatever reality it occupies. He has to use a tremendous amount of energy to sustain the effect. When it comes to the building, you'll see random lights on in certain offices at night even though it's supposedly abandoned. Those are the result of uncontrolled power surges. Once a vault is removed from the tower, it has a limited battery life. Given enough time, the box Kendell's stuck in will weaken its hold on her."

Myles's heart started beating so fast he broke into a cold sweat. "Once the cage loses its power, her soul in hell can reunite with her body in life through the seventh gate. She's already proved that's possible when she sent my soul back to my body after we tricked Colin into returning to hell. But if he knows about the upcoming power failure, he's likely to strike soon. He'll only have a limited amount of time to get what he wants."

Mary frowned while looking at the fire as if she were carrying on a secret conversation with herself and didn't like the response. "Kendell's problem isn't just spiritually reconnecting with her body. It's also physical. From what you've told me, her body is next to the seventh gate in Delphine's shop, and her soul is in the vault. Her prison is out of phase, and by losing its power source, it will return to hell's dimension, but for Kendell, that kind of jump from out of phase to the dimension the vault's in could play hell with her psychic energy. If her soul can make it back to the seventh gate, she'll be okay, but she may need some help."

*Why is nothing ever easy?* "So we contact Sanguine and have her fly Kendell home."

"That might be doable if Kendell was simply weakened and could recognize Sanguine. Remember what I said about horror stories? Kendell would be the monster that was out of sync with her surroundings. Everything she saw would be like a drug-induced nightmare. What she could really use is someone taking the trip with her—someone who understands hell's structure and could lead her out of the vault and to the shop."

Lynn added more bourbon to her cup. "And what about the puppies?"

Kendell would follow Cheesecake to the ends of the earth, if the dog pulled in that direction, but Myles wasn't as certain that the puppies would have the same influence. "If we can get back to the gate in time, we can warn Kendell about what's about to happen. She can tell the pups to guide her back to Delphine's once they're free. Any idea of how long that vault will maintain power?"

Mary started collecting the bowls and cups. "You can't expect me to have all of the answers."

Polly helped Mary round up the cutlery. "I have a question. Why are you here? I mean you specifically. I realize there are other versions of you living different lives, but why have you chosen to be homeless?"

Mary smiled at her like a teacher whose student had figured some hidden truth. "Because if I hadn't followed this path, I wouldn't be here now to answer your questions. I had to do what I could to help save Kendell. But now that I've played my part, it's time you got back to rescuing our river angel."

Myles was being pulled in too many directions. Now that he knew Kendell's location, he needed to contact Sanguine. She could at least stand guard in case Colin got any bright ideas now that he was about to lose his hold on Kendell's soul. Then there was finding out from Luther how long the vault battery was likely to hold out. Though Mary had presented her information with conviction, Luther could be a sneaky bugger when it came to the inner workings of the World Trade Center. And of course, he had to have some way of finding and opening the vault. Most importantly, Myles needed to be ready to save Kendell once she was freed. He tried not to imagine her as a zombie girlfriend crawling out of the Mississippi.

Minerva led the way back to her VW. "Where to first?"

*Screw it.* "The swamp is much too far, so we'll have to trust that Sanguine can figure things out on her own. Talking to Luther about damn near anything results in a daylong philosophical discussion about nothing. I want to head out to the shipwreck."

"What good will that do?" Polly asked. "Even if we're there when the vault loses power, all we'll see will be the puppies. Since Kendell is only being held in spirit, she would appear as a breath of cool air on a humid day. And if Mary is right about her not being in her right mind, our presence might only confuse her."

Myles tried to stay positive, though he was finding it increasingly difficult. "At least we'll find out if we're too late. We'll pick up Professor Yates on the way. He's good with paranormal mechanisms. He can stand watch at the shipwreck in case the vault hasn't materialized. If we don't see it, we'll hightail it back to Delphine's so we can try to access the gate and warn Kendell. I just hope we're not already too late."

## 13

*S*anguine followed up on each of her river animals' leads regarding anything out of the ordinary they found. She sat on top of the ferry terminal, drying her wings after her latest dive into the Mississippi. So far, she'd discovered the remains of two paddle-wheel shipwrecks, the bones of a shark that must have gotten seriously lost before dying in the brackish water, and so many Mardi Gras beads that the river bottom glistened as if someone had dumped a barge full of glitter into the water—but no mysterious hole in the water created by something that wasn't there.

Following Colin like a stupid schoolgirl with a crush was becoming her last option. She hugged her legs to her chest and spread her wings in the sun. Resuming their relationship—especially now that she didn't have to hide in someone else's body—might loosen him up to discuss his plans. After a good fight, guys were often honest as a way of showing contrition, but that window of truth never lasted long. In Colin's case, she guessed he'd be really open for about five minutes before resorting to his secretive ways. Though meeting with him again was worth a shot to save Kendell, Sanguine predicted it would result either in sex or in her impaling him with her flaming sword.

A flock of seagulls worked the air currents behind a passing freighter. Though the gulls were never the most useful informants, due to their fixation on filling their stomachs, Sanguine hopped off the terminal roof and spread her wings to join them. A little mindless flight with the diving and flapping birds would clear out the thoughts of Colin.

The cool air felt good on her wings, even if the stench of the ship's engines made her sneeze. To avoid crashing into the river wake, she glided away from the ship toward the shore.

Off in the distance, she spotted the back of a man in a familiar black suit. Though Colin often wandered the path along the river, from his determined gait, she guessed this wasn't a walk of contemplation.

*I need to stay unseen. Maybe he'll lead me to Kendell. It's about time he made a move.* She spread her wings and drifted left over the levee. By keeping low over Decatur Street and using the buildings for cover, she stayed hidden from Colin. Between her, the animals, and the cardboard people she'd inhabited, she knew the vault wasn't along the French Quarter riverbank. When the three-story brick structures that defined the Quarter ended, she worked her way through the open-air French Market, trying to blend in with the tourists. It was only a week before Halloween, so her wings wouldn't attract unwanted attention—so long as she wasn't flying.

At the end of the stalls, she hid behind a concrete wall that separated the shops from the railway tracks and waited for Colin to catch up. He didn't even look away from the path ahead as he walked past the warehouses that lined the wharf on the other side of the tracks. *I know that look. He's on a mission.*

By sticking to the residential streets of the Marigny and Bywater, she was able to track his progress without detection, but when he cut inland at the Industrial Canal, she had to use her sword to break into an abandoned warehouse. When she felt it was safe to come out, she'd lost him.

With a quick nod and spread of her wings, she summoned the flock of gulls that were still diving and weaving for pieces of bread thrown by the ship's crew. Reluctantly, they became her spies along the river. Even mentally hopscotching from bird to bird, Sanguine nearly missed Colin sneaking through the grove of trees overrun with vines. She directed the flock to make one more pass over the area so she could map out her approach. *I'm coming, Kendell.*

~

THOUGH KENDELL WAS no fan of being scared, she wasn't much happier with sitting bored in the vault for days, waiting for Colin to make his move so she could release her pack of hellhounds. The puppies were enthusiastic accompanists, but their barking as she sang didn't hold a candle to Cheesecake's modulated howling. "I love you dogs, but your singing isn't going to cut it for the Scratchy Dog. I guess you'll just have to survive on your love and good looks."

From the way they jumped on her, she knew they hadn't taken the criticism personally.

The sound of someone futzing with the door made Kendell and the dogs spring into their action poses. "This is it. Remember, push the box into the door opening, and get your furry tails out of here. Once you're back to your hellhound personas, bite him in the ass."

She would probably pass out once the door opened—hopefully not for long—but if she could get one good lunge at the gap first, she might throw Colin off balance. Then the dogs could make their escape and have time to transform.

The moment she smelled the dank, musty aroma of the Mississippi river, she hurled herself at the metal hatch. The impact hurt her shoulder so badly she thought she'd knocked it out of joint, but she felt the door open. As she fell out of the vault and onto the boat cabin's floor, she was surprised to still be conscious.

Instantly, she wished she had blacked out. She'd prepared herself for seeing the sweet little puppies become ravenous bloodthirsty hellhounds, but the rest of the scene made her fear she'd escaped into some demon dimension. A line of flames cut through the blue-and-orange air overhead. Behind her, gigantic wings created hurricane-force winds that shattered the glass windows. An explosion of razor-sharp shards filled the air and threatened to slice to shreds anything they encountered.

"Get out, Kendell. Follow the dogs. I've told them to guide you back to Delphine's." The words echoed in the small cabin as if they'd come from the goddess herself. Each piece of airborne glass reflected the image of the angry deity.

Kendell tried to stand, but the floor rocked to the side, causing her to lose her footing and crash into a ship's wheel. She grabbed it for support, but it spun, casting her back to the floor.

"Do you honestly think I would give up so easily?" The man's voice was so loud it hurt Kendell's ears.

Bolts of lightning cracked from the hatch and did battle with the line of flames that passed uncomfortably close to the top of Kendell's head. Nothing made sense. The whole scene could have been painted by a drugged-out gutter punk. Doughnut Hole hunched low and snarled at her, baring his teeth. His sisters nipped at her feet.

"Get off your ass, and get out of here, Kendell!" The goddess's words caused Kendell to roll toward the ship's hatch. With each inch that she crawled along the teak deck, the blade-wielding avenging angel followed.

To avoid the melee above her head, Kendell lay facedown and squirmed out of the room like someone in a boxing ring who didn't want to accidentally get pummeled by the competitors. Outside, she was free of the flames and lightning bolts, but the terrain wasn't much better. Towering ghostly black figures with thousands of arms waved menacingly at her. She hurried on her hands and knees to the deck railing. Looking over the edge, she saw a thousand-foot drop to an ocean of fire.

Doughnut Hole lay on his stomach and forced his way under her as she cowered and moved away from the ledge. In desperation, she wrapped her arms around his body and closed her eyes. Like a racehorse that had been let out of the gate, he took off so fast she had trouble maintaining her hold. Against the sides of her legs, she felt his sisters running with him in tight formation. The sounds of the battle behind her fell away.

~

THE SMELL of ozone and smoke stung Sanguine's blazing eyes. She wasn't in the mood to listen to Colin's excuses. Her anger at him fed the flames of her sword like jet fuel. "I warned you, but you just wouldn't listen." She swung the broadsword like a Scottish highlander protecting her family.

"She was never in any danger." His excuse was as weak as his spine.

Her swing of the blade forced him to hit the floor. The leading edge embedded in the teak doorframe and sent flames up to the cabin's ceiling. "Yeah, she looked in perfect health." With a firm tug, she freed the sword for another swing.

He raised his hands, and a bolt of lightning crackled through the air from his palms. "I don't want to hurt you. This is insane."

She angled the blade to repel the blast of electricity.

"You've already hurt me and threatened my best friend, all over a stupid stick. So tell me again which one of us is insane."

To her surprise, instead of continuing his cowering, he got to his feet. "Then do it. Kill me. Run that flaming sword right through my heart, because it was never my intention to make you this angry. If we can't talk out our difference, I'd just as soon be done with this whole existence."

The flames extinguished as easily as if she'd flipped off the lever of a welding torch. "You don't really mean that. A part of you has been around for over a hundred years. There's no way you'd sacrifice your plan that easily for me."

He brushed the dirt and soot off his coat. "Do you really find it that remarkable? I've never come up against a woman like you. Not even Kendell provided as much of a challenge. Just look at you with your angel wings, faceted-jewel eyes, and flaming sword. When am I ever going to meet someone else I can call an equal?"

She laughed in his face. "You think yourself my equal? I don't see you flying anywhere."

"That's because you denied me that power. By the way, why was that? Were you afraid of a man who might be *your* equal?"

She had to hand it to him. Unarmed and at a flight disadvantage, he still held his ground. "You were getting a little too full of yourself. Every time I turned my back on you, you found a way of disappointing me. You're like a little dog who rips up the furniture if left alone for too long."

"Ever think maybe I just need a good woman to be my partner?"

"What I *think*," she said, "is that you're trying to trick me again by playing the emotion card. It won't work. And by now, Kendell will have made it back to Delphine's, so you've lost your leverage over Myles. You won't get that cane back."

He still had a smug countenance that she found offensive. "Losing Kendell might have been a setback, but no game is won with one move. Join me, and I'll teach you how to be the master at the game of life and death."

A trickle of flame lit up the hilt of the sword. "And go through life known as the devil's woman? No thanks."

Colin folded his arms and leaned against the charred wall of the cabin. "Then what do you want?"

Sanguine had always been content to live in the swamps and study the animals she'd called friends, but that had been before meeting Kendell. That crazy voodoo guitarist had put her on the path that had literally and figuratively given her wings. "What I don't want—"

He cut her off. "I don't care what you don't want. People are full of answers about what they *don't* want. Picking a path forward, though—that takes guts and imagination. Don't make me reconsider my impression of you by giving me the typical response of listing what you don't like. You've chased me all over hell, made plans to erase me from history, and on more than one occasion—including just now—threatened to end my life. I hope you're not just doing this to gain favor with your dead grandmother. I can tell from your sword that I spark something inside you. So tell me honestly: what do you want?"

She had to confess that he challenged her as well. She spread her wings as far as the walls of the cabin would allow. "Angels are supposed to help people become more than they are."

"That's a job description, not a life goal. Have you ever considered that your grandmother might have given you those wings as a way of *turning* you into an angel? Stop thinking in terms of what others want for you, and tell me who you want to be. Because if you're just acting on the will of other people, I'm talking to the wrong person."

She wished they were still battling with fire. At least then she would have the upper hand. "I guess I'm still searching for what I want. I've only been at this life for twenty-four years. With your vastly greater experience, what's your answer? And please don't say that damn cane."

"My conflict with the loas of the dead goes far beyond my possession of a magical stick. I promise you, my mission is worth multiple lifetimes. Hear me out without jumping to judgment. Once I've stated my case, if you still don't believe I should own the cane, I'll listen to whatever alternate plan you can devise. At this point, what have you got to lose?"

*I don't know, and that's what worries me.* "Only on the condition that you stop threatening my friends."

"See, you're learning from me already. Never agree to anything without getting something in return."

## 14

*M*yles sat in Delphine's back room with the band huddled around Kendell's body. They'd done all they could. The trip out to the shipwreck had revealed exactly nothing. If the vault was there, they had no way of detecting it. Professor Yates had agreed to stand watch, though Myles doubted he'd be able to do anything useful should the vault appear. Contacting Kendell through the open gate had been equally useless. She was truly a spirit adrift.

"I can't just sit around like this," Polly said. "Let's sing or something. Anything is better than this death watch."

"What should we sing?" Minerva asked as she picked up some ritual bongos from Delphine's shelf.

Lynn stood and walked to the voodoo totem. "It may not help, but I've been singing 'My Girl' to Cupcake. Every time I break into the Temptations classic, she comes running.

Since the pups are with Kendell, maybe they can lead her back here. They do have enhanced hearing."

As the band broke into four-part harmony, Myles closed his eyes to let his mind slip away, into the song. Even Cheesecake howled out her accompaniment. If the pups would respond to anyone, it would be their mama and their human companions.

Myles's enjoyment of the song was interrupted by the pack of three adorable Lhasa apso puppies busting through the retail shop as if they were still in their hellhound forms. Doughnut Hole jumped on top of Kendell's body as if he were playing king of the hill. To Myles's surprise and relief, Kendell sucked in a deep breath and sat upright, but the look of terror in her eyes quickly squelched his enthusiasm.

"It's okay, Kendell. You're home."

She bolted off the floor and backed up to the small room's farthest wall. "Where are my protector hounds? All I hear are screams, and everything around me is on fire. Make it stop."

Cheesecake ran up to Kendell and lay at her feet. Kendell continued to look around the room as if she were being attacked, but she bent down to pet the shaggy coat. "Cheesecake? My sweet girl. Don't leave me."

Delphine joined the group after sufficiently distracting her clientele from their pursuit of the puppies into the back room. "She's out of phase."

Myles had had enough of Delphine's useless contributions. "Tell me something I don't know—like how to fix her."

But it was Polly who took the lead. "Time to break out

'Bohemian Rhapsody.' I know we've never mastered it, but if anything will bring Kendell back into harmony, that number will."

Kendell's attention darted to every band member as they formed up around their leader. It was as if her senses were drug enhanced.

Myles put out his hands. "Make as few movements as possible. Just sing. Hopefully, she'll be able to focus on the words and let her inner magic bring her across."

Polly started out singing soft and low as if trying to calm a wild animal. The others joined in with the same degree of vocal caution. By the time the band got to the complex harmony, Kendell was struggling to sing along. In her state of fright, she spoke more than sang the words. Not until they were singing about Beelzebub did she fully synchronize with the band. When the song ended, she was no longer staring around the room in terror.

Myles rushed up and took her in his arms just as her strength failed. "I've got you, and I'm never letting go."

~

THE MORNING after reuniting body and soul, Kendell woke to the sun beaming through the French doors. Cheesecake and Doughnut Hole were lying at the foot of the bed like guardian lions protecting their mistress.

Kendell's memories of her time in Colin's vault were as scrambled as a beaten egg.

Myles brought in a tray filled with pancakes and coffee. "How are you feeling?"

"Like the devil stole my soul and played it like a cheap guitar. My mental strings are pretty frayed. You saved my sanity by sending the puppies." She reached down and rubbed Doughnut Hole's back. "You are your mama's boy. I don't know if even Cheesecake would have done a better job at rescuing my soul."

Myles set the tray on the bed and took one of the cups of coffee. "Do you remember anything useful?"

*Do we really have to go there right now?* But she knew, as always, that time was against them. She was free of the melee, but Sanguine would still be in the devil's sights. "Not much. He wants the cane, but you know that. My best guess is Sanguine was the angel beast that saved me with her flaming sword, but the battle isn't clear in my head."

Myles nodded as if he'd made a decision. "Though the cane belongs to me, I'd never do anything with it before consulting you. I'll give it to him if it'll end this madness. Sanguine said he promised to leave this dimension alone. At this point, that's good enough for me."

All she wanted to do was cuddle up with her dogs and Myles. "Colin has beaten me in every way I can imagine. I don't have any fight left in me. He's won. But that cane is our final negotiating chip. We have to hang onto it in order to back Sanguine's play. She's our last best hope."

"And if he's playing her like he's played everyone else?" Myles asked.

After days locked in an iron vault like a submariner who'd sunk to the ocean floor, she found that the sunshine and fresh coffee were working their magic on her spirit. "He's lost me as his hostage. That gives Sanguine the edge.

She also looked pretty intimidating wielding her sword of justice. If she says to turn over the cane, I'll agree with her request. But until then, I think we need to let her play her hand."

"I just wish I knew what hand she was playing. I worry she may be down to the queen of hearts."

Kendell struggled to sit up. "We need to talk to her, but obviously, I'm not risking the use of my gate again."

"We figured Colin had found a way to eavesdrop on any of the gates. We just need to keep mixing up our use of all seven of them to keep him guessing. The most secure way of talking to Sanguine would be over her gate. He can't break into the line of communication like he did with yours, since he used the curse for that, so he'll have to be with her in the swamp if he wants to bust in on our conversation. We can head out to find her once you feel up to it. There is, of course, the problem of finding her island."

Though the coffee was helping, Kendell still felt lightheaded. "I remember she left a canoe hidden in the reeds. But finding our way through the bayou is going to be a challenge."

"The band and I discussed the idea while you were trapped in Colin's vault, so I've had some time to think about what I'd do in Sanguine's place. She has to expect at some point we'll be headed to her gate. All we can do is go out there and hope she figured out a way to guide us to her island."

Kendell lounged in bed with the dogs while Myles rounded up the band. She hated feeling like an invalid, but having Myles take point while also waiting on her hand and foot wasn't the worst way to spend a morning.

Even though the canoe Kendell remembered only sat three people, the whole band insisted on coming along for the ride. She lay on the bench seat of the bus and rested her head in Myles's lap. Though noisy, the VW engine lulled her back to sleep on the hour-long ride out to the bayou. The sounds and vibrations assured her she was back among those she loved and directed her dreams away from nightmarish images of waking up between dimensions.

The VW quieted down just before a firm jolt brought Kendell back to full consciousness. "We're there already?"

Polly peered over the back of the seat. "You were snoring so loud I thought there was something wrong with Minerva's bus."

The ribbing by the bandleader added to Kendell's feelings of her life getting back to normal. "Being locked in a spiritual cage isn't as restful as you might think."

"Come on," Polly said. "The band decided I should go with you and Myles while the rest stand guard. With three gates represented, there's no way Sanguine will be able to ignore our call."

Even though Kendell was still feeling stiff from too many days of inactivity, the sun on her face and the fall breeze against her skin made her glad to be outside. While she stretched out her limbs, Myles walked upstream along the bushes, saplings, and reeds, in search of the canoe.

He jumped out of the brush and ran back to the gravel parking lot. "I don't want to alarm anyone, but there is a big fat gator lying next to the boat."

Kendell walked toward the riverbank. "Do you think he's a guardian or guide?"

"I think he's ten feet long with scary sharp teeth and didn't want to be annoyed with human questions."

Kendell wasn't particularly curious about swamp creatures, and after her experiences of the last couple of days, bravery wasn't an emotion she embraced. But if Sanguine had left some animal in charge, she couldn't have chosen a better intimidator than a gator. "Let me go talk to him. If he is Sanguine's ambassador, he should respond to my voice."

She didn't even get to the edge of the gravel lot, however, before a rustling in the weeds caused Myles to grip her around the waist. A quiet splash from upriver called forth all the members of the band. The alligator that emerged from the vegetation occupied nearly the entire width of the river. A rope trailed behind him, connected to the swamp-water-stained canoe. He had to swim thirty feet out into the lake for the boat to line up with the beach.

Polly kept behind Kendell and Myles. "Maybe I'll rethink coming with you two."

Kendell didn't waste any time in climbing into the front of the boat. "I've paddled upriver before. The journey is hard on the arms. If Sanguine is providing gator power for the trip, I'm not going to object."

Myles climbed into the back, leaving the middle seat for Polly. "We've trusted our lives to scarier creatures. Come on, Polly. You can't tell me this river lizard is any more impressive than Muffin Top when she goes all hellhound."

Polly gingerly stepped on the rocks that lined the

riverbank. As a woman who normally wore stylish dress shoes, her tentative steps indicated she didn't have full confidence in the brand-new tennis shoes. "If I slip into the water, you're buying me a steak dinner." She eyed the swamp monster. "Complete with deep-fried gator bites."

Once everyone was settled, the alligator swam around to pull the canoe upstream. Kendell felt like a little kid holding onto the sides of a giant cardboard box that her father was dragging around the yard. The gator's smooth swimming style didn't create a single ripple on the water. His powerful tail moved the narrow boat along much faster than Kendell and Myles had managed in their poor attempt at paddling under Sanguine's supervision. Myles used a paddle at the back of the boat to steer them into the middle of the waterway and out of the thick water hyacinths.

The alligator had them at the island in half the time it had taken to paddle that distance. Myles steadied the canoe with his oar while Polly tried to keep her balance and step onto the shore. "I hate small boats. If it isn't big enough for a full-sized cooler filled with beers, you can count me out. A yacht large enough to justify a bartender making mixed drinks would be even better."

"Noted," Kendell said while joining Polly onshore. "But you can see the logistical problems of getting such a vessel up this small winding river."

Myles was the last to get out. "Normally, I'd tie off the boat, but I don't want to overstep my bounds. Think Gatorboy will hang around and wait for us?"

Kendell held Myles's hand. "I'm sure he will, and if not, we can complain to Sanguine."

Polly picked her way through the vines and grasses as if she were avoiding Bourbon Street's potholes filled with unknown liquids. "Why am I out here again?"

Kendell couldn't help but rip the city girl just a little bit. "Scouting out locations for our next gig. Just imagine this place at night with all manner of swamp people getting their groove on."

"Not even if you filled the rivers with moonshine."

Myles poked at some thick elephant grass with a stick he'd been using to scare away any hidden snakes. "Where do you suppose Sanguine set up her gate?"

From the top of the island, Kendell could just make out the old swamp witch's cabin in the trees. "You don't think she used Agnes's old home?"

"That's just it—I do. But we were in hell and Sanguine had come out here to get her grandmother's permission before forming the gate." He pointed the stick at the cabin twenty feet up in the cypress tree. "That house wasn't always up in that tree. I'd guess Sanguine went back far enough in time to visit her grandmother before the hurricane moved the structure."

Kendell looked around the small meadow bordered with trees. "This wouldn't be the worst spot for a homestead."

He poked again at the tall stalks of the elephant grass. "That's what I was thinking. It feels like there might be a brick pier for a raised structure in the middle of these plants. Spread out and look around for the veve Sanguine would have drawn to complete the ceremony. If I were her, I'd have used something that would remain after the home was relocated."

"Like that pier?" Polly asked.

Kendell handed Polly a stick. "Just watch for snakes."

"Have I mentioned how much I hate this swamp?"

～

SANGUINE LOVED HER SWAMP. The plants, animals, and solitude felt a million miles away from the hustle and bustle of New Orleans. This was her sanctuary from Colin—a place to process her emotions where he wouldn't even think of visiting.

Lefty heaved his alligator body up the small incline to the field and snapped his iron-trap jaw.

"Really? You know how I hate visitors."

He blinked both his horizontal and vertical sets of eyelids and headed back into the reeds.

"If you and Righty let them in, it must be important." She dragged her feet through the knee-high grass like a girl who'd just been called in from playing to do her homework.

The veve she'd carved into the long-unused brick support was covered in wisteria blossoms—the only section of the maze of vines that snaked up every vertical surface to be in bloom.

She pulled at the thick knotted cords. *Why did I let Kendell talk me into being a part of these gates? It would have been so much easier to destroy Colin if I hadn't given in. She could have taken care of herself without my help.* But the unyielding cords of wisteria vines were like the emotions wrapped around Sanguine's heart—beautiful, tenacious, destructive, and in the end, desired.

She dusted off the dirt that had caked into the carving. "I'm here."

When Kendell, Myles, and Polly came into view, Sanguine wondered who'd been abducted this time.

Myles sat cross-legged on a patch of cleared dirt. "We wanted to present as united a front to you as we could manage. Without even knowing your plan, we support you completely. Running all these different agendas has only divided us and given Colin the upper hand. Tell us what you need, and we'll do our part."

If the image had been a television, Sanguine would have rapped it on the side to make sure it wasn't on the wrong channel. "So you're just giving up?"

Kendell put her hand on Myles's shoulder. "No, we're not giving up. All he meant was we're letting you take charge. I can't handle another confrontation with Colin. I just don't have it in me. And left on his own, Myles would probably get into a fistfight with the devil. I don't imagine that would end well. Polly and the band have done the best they can, but Colin proved even our gate system is no match for his cunning. You're all we have left."

Sanguine wasn't buying it. "And you've come all the way out to my island to tell me this?"

Myles playfully twirled a stick. "Only as a preamble. I didn't bring the cane the loas left me, but it's at your service. If it comes down to you or the walking stick, give him the damn thing and come home. We can live with his promise not to invade our reality again."

"You'd all better sit down for this."

They got comfortable, and Sanguine did her best to

explain Colin's plan for resurrecting the dead, putting minimal emphasis on how they were all to blame for creating a hell where he could enslave every human being.

Myles tossed the stick he'd been playing with into the bushes. "So that's why he wants the cane? I thought he was just after more power."

"What's more powerful than having people owe him their souls?" Polly held her arms tightly around her stomach as if the vines might turn into snakes and bite her. The pose, combined with her too-tight jeans and cotton shirt, made her look like a city girl who'd been forced out to the swamp on a school field trip.

Kendell sat close to Myles. "And what does he want from you?"

"I'd be Mother Nature to him as God. Though Grandmother built this realm, she gave me the keys to operating it." Sanguine spread her wings. "In hindsight, I guess having these things kind of tipped my hand as to my powers."

Polly looked as if she'd swallowed a bug and was trying to figure out what kind it was, based on the taste. "But the human projections in hell aren't your creation. Professor Yates, Delphine, and Luther Noire jointly built that reality overlay."

Sanguine had done her best to keep what few cards she had left secret from Colin. "He doesn't know everything, but since he has the vault, all he really needs is the cane to implement his plan. So far, he still thinks of me as naïve and easily read. He believes because we have a relationship, I can't lie to him."

"Do you have a relationship?" Kendell asked.

Sanguine suppressed her usual snarky response. "I haven't slept with him in this form, if that's what you're asking. But I won't deny that the feelings I have for him aren't as easily ignored as they used to be before he met me in person."

"What about the gates?" Polly asked. "Has he made any move on the fourth one in the bank?"

Sanguine was happy her grandmother's island was only being invaded with a hologram, but even that was too much, considering the emotions she still needed to process. "According to my animal spies, he did go to the bank. From what Colin explained regarding his plan, I think he wanted to put the fear of the devil into the loas of the dead. But I don't know if he talked to Baron Samedi. If he did approach the fourth gate, it wasn't intentional. Whatever is happening with the seven gates isn't part of his plan. It's as if our portals are sitting in his path like potholes and he keeps tripping into them."

From the way Polly fidgeted, she looked like someone who'd been caught cheating and didn't want to suffer punishment alone. "But he could have talked to his kids."

"He didn't bring back the pastel drawing that would have indicated he'd passed through the gate." Sanguine shrugged her wings. "If he did meet with them, maybe they didn't let him pass."

Myles picked up a rock and threw it toward the water. "But him going through the gate is just a matter of time. If he was able to convince his wife of his rehabilitation, how much more cooperative would he find his children?"

Kendell stopped him from throwing another rock. "We did what we could. We tried to see Baron Samedi. With that evil woman in tow, it's not a surprise the voodoo loa wouldn't show himself. But if he knew we were there, hopefully he got word to Baron Malveaux's kids."

Polly kicked at the dirt. "Or he thought you were there to encourage the kids to let Colin pass. After all, he's already made it through the first three gates, including mine. I knew having the fourth gate to hell match up with the seventh gate to Guinee was going to bite us in the ass one day."

Myles started pacing. "That means he'll be up to my gate any day now." He turned back to Sanguine. "Then he'll be coming after you. Sounds like he's already softening you up. And finally, he'll take on Kendell. The whole reason we're here is because he's proven he can best her."

Kendell took him in her arms. "Maybe allowing him to pass wouldn't be the worst choice. It's either have him in life as a normal person, or leave him in hell, where he truly becomes the devil."

"There isn't anything normal about him," Polly said.

"We don't really know what happens when someone is redeemed through all seven gates." From the way Kendell's voice rose in pitch and volume, Sanguine could see she was on a roll. "After forming the gates, we all made the journey to get out of hell, but as we were all guardians, the process was mostly just a technicality. I've passed between dimensions without the benefit of the gates or Samedi's cane. It's changed me. So what if Colin *is* playing us all so that he can go through the final gate? Redemption isn't supposed to be just going to a parole board and saying the right words. There's an expectation that the condemned have dealt with whatever desire spurred them to act. If he's lying to us, he might end up in as bad a shape as I was. And if he's being truthful, maybe going through the final gate and transitioning from hell to life will cleanse him."

"You're not really talking about him being baptized like a born-again Christian," Sanguine said. "Besides, getting him to pass through the final gates is not as simple as putting up a sign that says This Way Back to Life, and we can't just force him through the gates. He has to show up to each one on his own, and then he has to prove he's worthy. Since Colin is no longer interested in returning to life, he has no incentive to play your little game. The minute he figures out what's going on, all he has to do is *not* show up."

"Then why has he gone through the first three gates?" Polly asked. She never did pick up on what was happening the first time it was explained.

Sanguine really didn't have time for this foolishness. Though she knew Colin's objective, she didn't know how he intended to get the cane or why he felt so confident in his ability to subjugate Guinee. All this talk of gates back to life was just proving to be a distraction. "Other than the first gate, his passing through them has been an accident. As for getting through Mary's gate, I think it's pretty clear he only did that to capture Kendell. I don't know why he hasn't figured out what's going on. After all, he did break into our ceremony. He can be a little dense at times, especially when it comes to emotions. Maybe he doesn't really know where each gate is located. He did have to rely on his bat spies, after all, and he couldn't trace down each of their directions in the short time of our ceremony. But whatever is prompting him through the gates, I don't see him trying to defend himself to Myles. Assuming he does make it that far, is there even anything he could say to justify the fact that he possessed your body?"

Myles looked from Kendell back to Sanguine, his brow furrowed. "I can't say I'm excited about having to confront him, but if he were to show up, at least I would be in a position of authority. I don't know if I would let our nemesis pass or not. Having that guy back in life would mean I could never turn my back on him. Even if he weren't trying to take over as the devil, his actions toward Kendell alone are enough to make me want to end him each time we meet, but him being here would mean we'd have you back with us to help. Leaving him in hell hasn't proven to be a long-term solution. At least with Colin in purely human form, I'd have a fighting chance of beating him."

*Guys never can trust an old suitor when it comes to their women. You'll pass Colin on because Kendell wants you to, but that's okay because then he'll be mine to deal with.* "If he shows up out here in the swamp," Sanguine said, "I fully plan on telling him that he's down to me and Kendell when it comes to the gates back to life. He has a right to know what he's in for. No one should have someone else's idea of redemption forced on them simply because they're trying to be a better person. It'll be up to him to decide if he wants to return to the land of the living or remain in hell as the devil. As for his idea of resurrecting lost souls, I'll confess I see his point. People shouldn't have to die, and I've never been a fan of the loas of the dead. Everyone should have a say in what happens to them."

Kendell leaned down to stare into the connection. "You can't be serious about letting him harvest souls to populate his hell."

"All I'm saying is I see his point. And whether I agree with him or not, fighting with him isn't going to change his mind. He does listen to me, though. I may not be able to talk him out of his plan, but maybe I can be the advocate for each dead soul he approaches with his offer of life everlasting in hell. We all know how slippery he can be when it comes to talking someone into doing something that might not be in their best interest. Everyone deserves proper representation."

Myles got down on his knees. "So I'm guessing your agreement to return to the living after six months is out. Sounds like the only way you'll let Colin proceed with his plan is if you would be there to prevent him from truly becoming the devil."

*You're cleverer than I've given you credit for.* "If he passes through the seven gates—no matter what he becomes—I'll return to life. There wouldn't be any reason for me to stay here. But if he's determined to follow his plan, I need to stay and be the voice of reason. You must see that."

"Is there no third option?" Polly asked "Why don't we just keep the cane and leave him in hell?"

"Because he'll come busting back into life as the devil," Myles said. "We've already seen what happened to Kendell when she crossed dimensions without using one of the established paths that Mary laid out. Imagine someone who considered himself the devil going through that mind-altering process."

Sanguine ruffled her wings. "There's also no guarantee that he wouldn't retain his devilish powers. I'm able to keep them in check here in hell because this is my grandmother's realm. Back among the living, I wouldn't have that kind of control. He'd be like the puppies when they transform into hellhounds, only in Colin's case, he's reasonable in hell and a monster in life. As much as I hate to say it, keeping him locked up here like he's in a cage just isn't an option. We're down to his redemption or escape, or our surrender."

From the way Kendell arched her back, she seemed ready for a fight, but the movement lasted only a moment. "As Myles said, we're behind you no matter your decision."

# 15

---

*C*olin sat in his loft and watched the paddle wheeler pull out from its dock. He felt like a riverboat gambler who'd just lain down his cards. All that was left was for his opponents to show theirs so they could figure out who had won. Unfortunately, at the moment, he was the only one sitting at the card table.

Though Colin had lost control of Kendell's soul, Myles would be desperate to prevent another threat to her—perhaps enough to take Colin's offer of steering clear of life in exchange for ownership of the cane. *Eventually, that fool has to figure out he's no match for me.* Even if Colin did somehow lose this hand to Myles, they both still had chips on the table. If he'd read Myles correctly, the man would be counting what he had left to lose. A true gambler knew—whether winning or losing—to read his opponent in times of crisis, not measure the stack in front of him.

Kendell was a worthier opponent, but as was often the case with reckless players, after she'd gone all in, he knew he had her. She'd need one hell of a hand to stay in the game. She'd gambled well, and he would miss her savvy way of playing her cards, but in the war of attrition, she'd lost more than she could afford.

The strongest competitor was Sanguine. They'd gone hand for hand, and he still didn't know her strategy—or even how many chips she had left. As the one overseeing his hell, she had an undue advantage, but Colin had never decried how the deck had been shuffled, and he had no intention of showing weakness now. There had been plenty of times in life when he'd controlled the way the cards were dealt. Lack of fairness was just a part of the game.

His bigger concern involved his feelings for her. She held the advantage over their relationship. He desperately wanted something more, and she knew it. What she wanted, however, eluded him. *It's going to come down to just the two of us. The sooner the rest drop out of the game, the better.*

The loas of the dead were a no longer an issue. By threatening Baron Samedi, Colin had ensured that word would spread throughout Guinee about the devil's impending return. The loas could be a gossipy bunch when they weren't competing for control. His message would work its way to Baron Kriminel. There was bound to be a battle once Colin returned to the voodoo purgatory, but as Baron Malveaux, he'd had a hundred years to learn each of the loas' weaknesses. *I'd best not get ahead of myself.*

With Myles and Kendell off licking their wounds and Sanguine playing her card of emotional distance, Colin grabbed his coat and headed out to the river to consider his next move. The cool breeze off the river always helped him focus on the world around him. It was such a short walk to the nearest bench that he considered it part of his backyard.

He pulled his coat up around his neck and sat on the cold metal to watch the water. Using the cane to maneuver souls from Guinee to hell involved the fewest unknowns in completing his plan. But getting hold of the cane had proven more difficult than he'd hoped. Relying on Sanguine's love for him being strong enough for her to convince Myles of his inevitable loss was becoming a long shot. Colin needed to start working on a fallback plan. Finding time alone was always a problem. If he and Sanguine did become a couple, he'd have precious little privacy to work on his creation undetected. Without the cane, the problem—as always—was amassing enough power in the vault and having the ability to control it.

His vault had only lasted a few days with its battery backup. Even when activated, the damn box wasn't controllable. At the very least, he needed an on-off switch. A power dial would be even better. Capturing souls from one dimension and releasing them in another would take finesse. *First I need a source of power. There's no point worrying about the controls if I don't have a way to make the system work.*

Once the power problem was solved, he needed to reconfigure the vault to connect to Guinee. From there, snatching souls from the voodoo loas of the dead would amount to little more than proper advertising of his club along Afterlife Street. No one really wanted to die. They just didn't want to get sick, feeble, or aged. Bringing them to his dimension would solve the problem of the fate humanity had feared for all of its existence. Bowing down to the devil would be a small price to pay for escaping death. With eternity in front of him, he'd own every human soul by the time he was done. But first he needed to confirm that a soul could be transferred into one of hell's human puppets.

The river current swirled from the conflicting forces of incoming tide and melting snowpack from far upstream. Though powerful, the moving water would be hard to transform into a means of running his vault.

He kept his back to the World Trade Center. Obviously, all the little people and actions in his hell were being powered by the paranormal generation field he'd created in that tower, but the controls weren't accessible. *I need a way to tap into that power source.*

A family with three little children walked between him and the river. He watched the youngest daughter skipping along the concrete path. *Could the answer really be that simple?* He pulled out his cell phone and called for his town car.

The family was a good hundred yards away by the time he saw the elegant black vehicle working its way through the parking lot. He signaled to the driver to follow along on the narrow access road that was used mostly for emergency vehicles and deliveries.

As he walked far enough behind the family not to be noticed, he tried running the computations. He didn't really need to power up the vault for it to work its magic. He only needed it as a doorway between dimensions. The real energy source was the relationship between the human soul and an empty voodoo-powered body. He just needed to establish the connection as if he were wiring up a piece of metal to opposing battery terminals.

The family was busy reading every touristy sign they ran across as the little girl mindlessly skipped farther ahead unattended. *She's not real, just a projection. Besides, who's going to stop me?* As he passed the two adults, he tossed a handful of coins off the side of the path like someone feeding breadcrumbs to pigeons. The two remaining children dove on the money that had scattered between the rocks of the levee. Once the parents turned to investigate the reason their little ones had scampered over the edge and toward the river, Colin made his move. He had the little girl under his arm and in the back seat of the town car before her cries had a chance to alert her parents as to the abduction.

He covered the girl's mouth with his hand and yelled to the driver, "Take us over the Industrial Canal, and be quick about it."

At any moment, either of the two human puppets in the car might be taken over by Sanguine, and Colin would end up with way too much explaining to do. He had to move fast. The long black car wove down the narrow streets, avoiding pedestrians and parked delivery trucks. The child squirmed in his arms, but her actions were more like those of a fish caught in a net than a human figuring out a way to escape. A rumbling under the wheels let Colin know they were crossing the bridge. They'd be at the vault in a few minutes. "Relax, little girl. I'm about to give you your heart's desire. Haven't you ever heard the story of Pinocchio?"

Dragging her out to the partially submerged wreck took

more strength than he'd have imagined, but once in the wheelhouse, he tossed her into the vault and shut the door. Without the power to keep the vault in its interdimensional realm, the normal latches once again worked easily. He threw the large lever and dogged the hatch shut. "You won't have to be in there for very long. I promise. Just don't hurt yourself." *Or that body.*

He pulled the pipe tool out of his pocket and waved it around the door, feeling its energy. Like a magnet calling to others like itself, the corresponding power from his cursed items locked itself in the vault with the girl. *Step one completed.*

His suit was soaked from working through the hip-deep water to the boat. Falling over the edge on the way back to the town car didn't help, but it wasn't as if he could get much more uncomfortable. The driver stood calmly beside the open door as if Colin had just come out of Commander's Palace. "Back to the condo?"

"No. Take me to the bank. There's someone I need to talk to." Colin feared that saying anything more would call forth Sanguine. He'd been lucky so far. *She must be really pissed if she's still holed up with her emotions.*

He twirled the pipe tool nervously as they made the short drive back to the Quarter. The first test of stealing Kendell's soul had worked better than he'd expected. That proof of concept was enough to risk step two, though what he had planned wasn't going to get him everything—or everyone—he wanted. The biggest challenge was the vault. With his possessions inside, he should be able to snatch anyone associated with the curse, but that was a very limited number of people. Ultimately, he needed a much bigger connection to human souls, but he needed to work methodically. The first challenge was bringing a human soul into his realm in a physical form.

*It won't be long now, my sweet Serephine.*

# BOOK LIST

# ABOUT THE AUTHOR

G.A. Chase is the pen name for Greg Chase. He is a science fiction and paranormal author living in New Orleans with his wife, fellow author Deanna Chase, and their two shih tzu dogs. On any given day you can find him behind his computer, people watching in the quarter, or out in his studio creating stories in glass. His glass work can be found at www.chase-designs.com.

www.gregchaseauthor.com

www.ingramcontent.com/pod-product-compliance
Lightning Source LLC
Chambersburg PA
CBHW020324200626

46814CB00006BB/2410